Spring Tales

Ruler's Wit

Copyright rests with the individual authors.

Published March 2016.

Publisher: Ruler's Wit

ISBN-13: 978-1530762439
ISBN-10: 153076243X

All rights reserved. No part of this publication may be reproduced, stored in a retrieval system, copied in any form or by any means whether electronic, mechanical, photocopied or recorded or otherwise transmitted without written permission from the publisher. You may not circulate this book in any format.

The moral right of the authors has been asserted.

Contents

Waiting for Spring - *Donna Shepherd* — 5
Promise of Adventure - *Melinda Ingram* — 14
Debt to Karma - *Stephen Ashurst* — 32
Spring Brake - *Karen Ette* — 39
No Ball Games - *Donna Shepherd* — 47
Bluebell Woods - *Melinda Ingram* — 66
Laid at my Feet - *Stephen Ashurst* — 76
Dance with the Daffodils - *Karen Ette* — 85
A Gift in Spring - *Donna Shepherd* — 106
Betrayal - *Melinda Ingram* — 118
Far From Here - *Stephen Ashurst* — 125
Elephant in the Room - *Karen Ette* — 144

Waiting for Spring
Donna Shepherd

Jenny glanced up at the loft hatch in the ceiling above her head as she pulled the bedroom door shut behind her. Stepping down onto the landing, she remembered how the step up to each bedroom had made them laugh as they had frequently tumbled into the rooms. They'd discussed replacing the old loft ladders with a staircase, but the thought of all that mess and dust had made her shudder. She had promised herself that she would go up there; a small part of her even thought that sifting through his things would help, but another Christmas had passed and her determination had melted away just like the snow that had arrived last month.

Tears rose unbidden in her eyes as memories washed over her and shuddering Jenny sat down heavily on the step behind her.

Six years since James had died. Six years since her lying, cheating, shit of a husband had killed him. Five years and eight months since Craig had been sent to prison.

It had just been another New Year's Eve party. The same as she and Craig had held every year. The house lit by candlelight, full of friends and family. James, had just turned twelve and to celebrate he'd invited his friends round for a mammoth session on his new

PlayStation. Jenny had kept an eye on him. "It's what parents do," she had informed him after he'd grumbled at her vigilant observation. "And besides, you're still my baby," she'd added, much to his obvious mortification. Laughing, she'd moved away, leaving him alone with his mates in the games room.

Jenny groaned and leant back against the wall. That evening had been the last time she'd seen him. Alive, anyway.

Later on, much later, she'd been told that there was someone at the door for her. Jenny remembered how she had been laughing with her best friend Jude, champagne in hand, before she had walked out of the lounge. The woman at the door was a stranger, but only to Jenny. She had introduced herself as Rebecca and proceeded to tell Jenny, right there on the doorstep, that she was having an affair with Craig. It was serious and she wanted Jenny to do the right thing and give him up, for James's sake.

Jenny remembered laughing, slightly too loudly, and calling Craig's name. He'd appeared from the kitchen, the smile frozen on his face at the sight of the two women by the front door.

She'd expected denial, but had got simple admission. Craig's face had revealed all and the triumph on the other woman's face had stripped Jenny of all coherent thought. Jenny had started screaming, stopping only when Jude had wrapped her tightly in her arms.

Rebecca had backed away from the front door and Jenny heard Craig say that he would follow her later. The door had closed and Jenny had fallen to the floor, Jude's arms still in place and holding her tight.

"Why, why, why?" she had yelled, "What have you done?" she'd asked between her sobs.

Craig had stared at the floor, unable or perhaps unwilling to meet her wretched gaze. His silence had motivated her to action. Standing, she had grabbed the vase of flowers from the hall table and hurled it at him. The resounding crash had made him jump but still no words. She had flown at him, demanding answers, oblivious to the people around her who simply didn't know what to do.

She remembered James's tear-stained face staring up at her, asking through his hiccups why she was shouting. Craig had left, insisting that he be the one to have James until she had calmed down. Jenny was in no fit state to look after their son, he had told their guests. She'd watched as he'd hastily bundled James into the front seat before driving off, the tail lights of the Jaguar blinking down the track.

Jenny pushed her head back onto the wall and stared up at the ceiling, dragging in deep lungfuls of air as the tears coursed freely down her face.

The house had emptied until it was just her and Jude, sitting facing each other. A single candle burned in the middle of the table. Jenny held a cup in her hand and gazed into its murky contents. "Coffee with something for the shock," Jude had said. They'd sat for hours that way. Both women had been blissfully unaware that the worst was yet to come.

At four in the morning Jude had risen and helped Jenny to her feet. "You must try and sleep," she had said. "James will be home tomorrow and you need to be strong for him."

They were walking towards the staircase, arms wrapped around each other, when the doorbell sounded for the second time that night.

Jude opened the door. Looking back at Jenny she'd stated "it's the police," as two uniformed officers walked into the hallway.

The larger policeman had steered her towards the conservatory and helped her into one of the seats. Taking his place opposite her, he'd said "there has been a car accident, Mrs Watson. I'm afraid it's serious…."

Jenny remembered the roaring in her ears as the kindly-faced policeman had told her that her husband was critically injured and that her son was dead.

The house was soon full of strangers, strangers in uniform asking her questions, so many questions; about the husband who had left her and the son who had been taken away from her.

The doorbell rang. "Oh shit," Jenny said, fumbling in her jeans pocket for a tissue. She scrambled to her feet and ran to the window that overlooked the drive. Pushing the cream voile to the side, she gazed down at the path below.

The postman, Tony, gazed back up and waved.

Taking a deep, calming breath, Jenny returned his wave and let the voile slip back into place. She walked down the stairs, forcing a smile onto her face before opening the front door.

"Morning, love," said Tony. "Quite a bit for you today," he continued, as he passed her a pile of envelopes.

"Thanks, Tony," Jenny replied, accepting the mound with both hands.

"Oh and there's a rather special looking one here too," Tony said as he pulled a cream coloured envelope from his bag. "Looks like a posh invite if you ask me," he chuckled.

"I've really no idea," she said, "but I hope it's something nice." Jenny glanced up at the darkening sky. "That looks ominous," she commented, "I'd best get in and let you get on with your round. Thanks again, Tony," Jenny said as she stepped back into the hallway and closed the door behind her.

The smile slid from her face as she dropped the stack of post onto the hall table with a thud, and then walked through the archway into the light and airy kitchen with the cream envelope in her hand.

Turning the kettle on, she put a spoonful of coffee into a mug, and then went and sat in the conservatory to wait until it boiled. Placing the envelope on her lap she looked at the handwriting. It was addressed to her and the postmark said Birmingham. Craig was in a prison in Birmingham. Jenny sat back in the chair and absentmindedly gazed out of the windows. Spring was edging its way past the winter, little green buds forcing their way out of the soil, and soon the borders would be full of her favourite yellow and purple crocuses.

The garden had provided her with a focus after James's death; she had spent hours digging everything up and then planting whole new swathes of colour. The physical exertion had forced, even temporarily, the policeman's words from her mind.

Craig had been driving too fast, the policeman had said, and while attempting to overtake, had lost control of the vehicle. Striking the kerb, the car had ploughed into on-coming traffic. James hadn't stood a chance and neither had the old couple in the other car. Craig, on the other hand, survived.

Leaning forward she picked the envelope up and tore it in two. She then placed both halves on the table in front of her, sliding the contents of each out. Craig's spidery handwriting covered the two bits of paper. After a cursory greeting, he'd thanked her for the offer to stay and given the date and time of his release. Jenny glanced at the calendar on the wall – two weeks today and he'd be free.

It seemed insensitive that he would get out of prison in time for the spring. New life everywhere, tarred with his imminent release.

Jenny blinked and wiped the angry tears from her cheeks. What had hurt the most, and still burned deeply in her gut, was the fact that Craig had loudly informed their guests that she was unfit to care for James in the safety of his own home. Despite consuming a large quantity of alcohol, Craig had chosen to take James away in the car.

He was coming back – the law simply hadn't done enough. Taking a deep breath, she got up, made herself a coffee and walked through the doors into the garden. Picking up the gas bottle from the shed, she made her way towards the caravan, which sat blocking the gate at the end of the garden. The door opened with a groan, the smell of damp assailing her nostrils. "Yes," she said to herself, "this will do nicely."

*

The sound of a key rattling in the lock made Jenny jump.

"Jenny," Craig called through the letterbox, "Let me in, love."

"I'll give you bloody love," Jenny muttered darkly, striding into the kitchen. Grabbing a set of keys and pulling on her wellies, she slammed the back door shut behind her. Yanking the gate open, Jenny called his name and then stood just inside the garden. Craig appeared, smile in place. "Hello," he said, "my key doesn't seem to work."

"No, it wouldn't," Jenny replied coldly, seething at his easy manner. "You won't need a key," she added and keeping her distance from him, she started to walk down the garden path.

Craig dropped his bags on the floor. He tried the back door and found that locked too. "What's going on?" he asked, "I'm tired and I just need something to eat, a hot bath and my bed." He glanced at the floor, "look love, I know we have to talk and we will," Craig spread his hands in what Jenny recalled was his placating gesture. Now it just made her want to bury a spade in his neck.

Fixing him with a withering stare, Jenny pointed to the old caravan at the end of the garden. "That is your new home," she said. "I won't have you in the house, ever. Do I make myself clear?"

Craig cleared his throat. "Look, Jen, I know I messed up, with Rebecca and James, but you can't expect me to sleep in that old thing? Bloody hell, it should have been condemned years ago."

"How apt, "Jenny muttered as she stalked past him.

"Fine," he shouted to her retreating back. "But only for tonight and tomorrow we will talk – about everything."

Breathing deeply, Jenny opened the back door and slammed it shut in his face, sliding the bolt across as she did so.

*

The explosion rocked the house. Jenny scrambled out of bed and ran into the back bedroom, which was lit with flickering orange.

"Ha, so he was right," she sniggered, surveying the bits of caravan strewn around the garden. "But it would have been a shame to condemn it before serving its purpose."

Promise of Adventure
Melinda Ingram

"Are you ready, then, Ellen? Everything's sorted for the party tonight so we can go out now."

"Do we haaaave to?"

"Yes, we do! You know we all enjoy visiting interesting old places, and while we're here in Loughborough we might as well make the most of it. The Town Trail sounds really good."

Ellen's family were staying at Caravelli's in Sparrow Hill, which used to be called "The Old Manor." Dad booked it after reading on the internet that it was supposed to be one of the oldest buildings in the town. He'd got stupidly carried away, enthusing about the fine Swithland Slate roof and the central gable, or something. Building materials? Boring! How people lived was much more interesting so Ellen was quite excited to hear they had recently discovered a fourteenth century fireplace, and the rooms were all oak beams, stone walls and four poster beds.

There were only four rooms in the hotel, all named after Lords and Earls who had lived there in the old days. Theirs was Huntingdon. She had googled the family straight away, and after a bit of digging she'd discovered that the seventh Earl of Huntingdon had had loads of kids and had lived in the manor house during the 1600s, a coincidence she felt oddly pleased about. It fitted nicely with game she'd been playing on her phone for the last week or so, which was all about spotting items in pictures of a house during the Restoration. Ellen's family had been invited to a posh do in the Italian restaurant at the hotel the next day. It was Nana Kate's ninetieth birthday party. Dad had got one of those offers for a mini break and because of the party he suggested making it a long weekend. It was alright though because it was spring bank holiday so there was no school. Ellen heaved a dramatic sigh.

"Okay, I'm coming," she said, putting down the game and leaning into the gap between the bed and the casement windows to retrieve ankle boots with leather laces which she teamed with leggings and a longish cream coloured shirt. Ellen looked into the oval mirror on the dressing table, scraping her shoulder-length hair back into a hair tie. She gave the shirt a tug or two around the top of the arms and then shrugged on a sleeveless black woollen jerkin, dropping her iPhone into the right hand pocket. It was a crisp spring morning, and the sun was shining, so Ellen didn't mind going really. The Town Trail included a visit to the Old Rectory Museum on Steeple Row, which was only open on Saturdays...lucky it was Saturday today!

"Sensible footwear, good! We'll be doing a bit of walking," said her Dad. "It'll be an adventure, I promise."

*

Ellen's parents headed down the stairs, which opened into the hall opposite the restaurant. Ellen followed, running her hand over the smooth, curved, wooden banister. It was quiet as breakfast was over, and the staff were getting ready for a lunchtime pasta event. Ellen loved pasta, but she wouldn't have been able to manage it just yet after their full English breakfast. She usually only had porridge, and sometimes got away with just toast and juice. Mum was holding a copy of the Town Trail.

"Where do we start, Mum?"

"Here. We've been to antique fairs in the Town Hall and we know the market well. Today Dad and I thought we would concentrate on old Loughborough."

Soon they were on their way down the quaintly cobbled street, passing the old guildhall, which was a hospital ages ago according to the guide, the church and a long row of little cottages, built along the left hand side of the road.

"I reckon the Old Rectory is behind this wall." Dad flicked his thumb out at the high red bricks running all the way down the right of Steeple Row. Ellen took a couple of running steps and jumped as high as she could to see over. Hmm! A neatly lawned garden and trees covered in pink blossom, probably soon to be apples. The gate at the end of the road was open and a long gravelled path led up to their goal.

"This was probably the original orchard garden," said Mum, reading. "It says here that most of the original house was demolished by the council a few years back now. What a shame!" They stared at what was left, so much smaller and perhaps older that they had been expecting.

Ellen walked quickly so that she reached the entrance to the museum first. Pushing open the modern glass door, she thought how strange it looked against the enormously thick walls that seemed to be made from boulders of many different sizes. How clever to have constructed the walls finding just the right stone to fit in each gap! The arched windows stretched from floor to ceiling.

"Mum, do you think the windows would have been that big in the old days?" Ellen asked.

"Probably not," came the answer. The lady behind the counter that served as a reception and mini-shop overheard her question and came over. "Your Mum is right," she said. "At times windows were taxed according to number and size, so these would almost certainly have been about half the depth they are now. You'll notice the flag-stoned floor, too. The Council decided to take the decor back to how the building would have been in medieval times when they restored it to be used as a museum."

"Oh yes, Mum was reading about that. What part of the house was this bit then?"

"We think this was the kitchen and servants area. Do look around. There are quite a few artefacts you can touch and read about, and you can go upstairs where there are more things on display."

The lady went back to her papers on the desk and looked busy. Mum and Dad were well into things already, totally engrossed. They were reading everything. Ellen wandered over to the far corner, away from what seemed to be a central fireplace, towards the stairs in the corner of the room. They seemed to be pulling at her like a magnet. Leaving her parents behind, Ellen started up the modern open metal circular staircase which rose into the room above.

"Watch out for the ghost," the lady called after her, looking up from her work.

"Yeah, right!" Ellen thought, but she looked back down and smiled.

Just inside the room she read from a poster about a lady called Elizabeth, who had married the rector in 1661. It caught her eye because it was about the 1600s like her game, and mentioned fighting between the Cavaliers and Roundheads. For a while Cromwell's Roundheads had been winning, Ellen remembered from lessons at school. King Charles had been chucked out and had to leg it to France. Apparently this Liz had married her gentleman, Mr Hall, just after he'd got his land back when Charlie boy was restored to the throne. Lucky Charlie, lucky Mr Hall and hopefully, lucky Liz, too. "Hmm, not sure about being the second wife though," Ellen murmured. The rest of the story was too much to read. She turned slowly, eyeing the room. The corner opposite where she was standing wasn't a corner at all. It had been built across in a strange way and as she looked she noticed the tiny opening only just big enough for a person to pass through.

"Why's the corner of the room chopped off like that," she thought. "And what's that thing for?"

A metal grille covered the opening, obviously to stop people stepping out into nothing. As Ellen drew closer she could see the remains of a circular staircase built in stone, in the corner of the building. There had been a door once because the old metal fixings still stuck out uselessly from the uneven nobbled edges. Some of the stairs, the ones near the doorway, had crumbled. Ellen looked down through the hole formed by the missing stairs. So many people must have made their way down the spiral staircase to the outside, perhaps to the garden, or the kitchens…or trudged upstairs to rest, over the centuries.

The stairs that remained were worn, gnarled in places, and so very narrow. A window at the turn had been cemented in. The turning post in the centre had chips and scrapes made from so many journeys, so many hands holding on as they passed by. Ellen took out her phone, and scrolled to the camera icon, pressing the button. The camera flashed with a pinkish light. That was odd! Ellen checked the picture file, but there was no photo. Hold on, though! She could hear sounds…chopping, a voice calling. She shook her head in an effort to get rid of the ringing that had started in her ears and leant over the metal grille for a better look.

"Wait a moment," Ellen whispered to herself. "No hole!"

"That wasn't the way they were just now," she said more loudly, stepping back a pace and, closing her eyes to get rid of the dizzy feeling. Her ears were ringing. The stairs had repaired themselves!

After a moment she opened her eyes again and cautiously peeped at the stairs through the grille. Yep, the space **was** there, a gaping hole and no stairs. The stones were old and gnarled again, but just now the walls had been smoother and cleaner looking, hadn't they? And she thought she'd glimpsed a looped rope handrail.

"I'm going mad," she thought. She backed away and turned round. "That didn't happen. I'm being stupid. Act normal, Ellen."

Still holding her phone, Ellen snapped off a couple of shots around the room, the usual bright yellow flash marking each one. She noticed that there must have been an old fireplace on one wall – you could still see where the hearth would have been. There were a few items of clothing on display. One dress was quite nice, but some of the things were a bit "pasta their besta," as Dad would say. "They've been around for a while, I suppose," she thought looking at the boots, that weren't unlike her own. There was a bit on the wall about people in Loughborough making woollen stockings. And they mostly didn't wear pants. Emma could think of some people now who would be glad to avoid a panty line, but in those days with the long swirly skirts there'd be no need to think like that. She tried to prolong her panty musing but she knew she was just putting off what she had to do.

"I'm going to have to have another look," she said to herself, "but first I'd better just check where Mum and Dad are."

Ellen leaned over the railing of the stairs she had come up. She could hear her Mum and Dad deep in conversation with the lady at the counter. Something about how the history group that met in this place had managed to save it from being completely flattened. They'd be there a while. Ellen turned and approached the corner of the room once more. She wanted to look but almost didn't want to look at the same time. She swallowed. She clenched her hands into fists. Could she? Should she? She stepped forward and leaned a little way out with her finger on the camera button. Pink light! Faint ringing in her ears. Someone was calling her name.

"Ellen...Ellen, where art thou?" Ellen's eyebrows shot up.

"Whaaat? Art thou? Who talks like that? Someone must be having a laugh."

She turned her head and looked back, but it wasn't her Mum. Whoever it was doing the calling was down the stone stairs she'd seen. She leaned in again. Thwack! She was hit from behind, pushed forward by the door which hadn't been there and now was. It had swung to, knocking her onto the stairs, the stairs that hadn't been there and now were. She looked at her feet on solid stairs with rounded eyes. Her heart was thumping. She turned and stared at the door which had closed behind her, her mouth opening and closing with little gasps, like a fish out of water.

"I don't believe it," she said, stretching out her hand to touch the newly appeared, and new looking door set in the clean stone walls.

"Ah, here thee art," said a voice. Ellen turned and saw a girl about her age coming up the stairs.

"Thee found our room, then?" she asked, pushing open the door that had surprised Ellen so much just now. "Come on, Clay-brain. Thee can't be working half dressed. Thee's a working woman now. I'm Jayne, by the by. Thee'n me'll be working together, in the kitchen and the laundry."

It was a good job that Jayne hadn't stopped talking, because Ellen couldn't have spoken if she'd tried. Her throat felt dry, and she felt as if she must have a really soppy sort of look on her face as she followed Jayne into the room she had come from. Only now there was a fire place and four low beds. Jayne went to a box with a lid at the end of one of the beds and Ellen watched as she lifted out some material.

"Here be a skirt, an apron and a head square until thou has thy own. The Missus gave them to me last week, and I mended the tear. Thee can hardly see it."

Ellen stood still in the middle of the room.

"That be where thee'll sleep, over there, with me," Jayne pointed.

Ellen turned around slowly, in the direction Jayne had indicated, hoping to see the stairs she had come from at first, hoping for anything that seemed familiar. But one of the beds (their bed?) was in that corner of the room.

"I don't know what's happened, I don't understand," she said in a low voice.

"Thee'll know what's happened if thee don't move quickly. We'll both be for it. There's the washing to do and the tatties for tonight."

She came towards Ellen, flapping open the skirt.

"Pull this over thy shift."

Ellen allowed Jayne to help her tie the skirt fixings and she pulled the apron over her head tying it behind her, under her woollen jerkin. As she tied the square over her hair and knotted it at the base of her head in the same way as Jayne was wearing hers, she was thinking "Hang in there, Ellen, just go along with it for now. Everything will go back to normal in a minute."

"Commmme oooon, Clay-brain," Jayne said, taking Ellen's hand and pulling her towards the door once more. As they ran down the stairs Ellen slipped her hand into her pocket and cradled her phone. She'd have to keep it out of sight. She'd been promised adventure but this was more than she'd bargained for.

*

"Tain't far now. See, there's the swans making their way t'pool at t'back of Guild," Jayne told her as they walked arm in arm.

They'd left the kitchen of the Rectory, the kitchen that had been so strange with its open hearth, great lumps of meat curing in the chimney, and its cooking pot over the fire. Jayne? Well, Jayne had become a friend. Ellen had tried, really tried, to find the words to tell her that she wasn't from this time. Jayne had only understood that she had been living "abroad" for a while, which explained why "her ways were different," and why Ellen needed her guidance!

This was just the sort of day Ellen usually loved. It was a crisp spring morning, very like Saturday had been. Yellow daffs waved amongst the grass and the trees were full of pink blossoms just the same. The sounds were different though. There were no road noises, no mobiles beeping. There was quacking, hissing, barking, mooing, baaing, the creaking of cart wheels, horse hooves clicking, all mixed in with the sounds of people going about their lives. The smells were different, too. No traffic fumes, but plenty of "farrrm smells." Probably even too many for her Dad's liking, Ellen thought, as she pictured her Dad taking in deep breaths, encouraging her to do the same during their country walks.

"Get that there country air deep in your lungs," he'd say. "Nothing like it!" Tears pricked at her eyes, and she wiped them away on the edge of the woollen wrap that she wore crossed over her clothes and tied behind her.

Jayne's constant chatter kept Ellen informed as she did her best to keep up. Her long skirts wrapped themselves around her legs. Her boots wobbled on the stony, muddy path (road?), so it was a good job they were flat. The lane reminded her of the track through the woods near where Ellen's family lived. Here, though, it was the main way into town. Other people were going the same way, laughing and calling to one another. It was market day, so Jayne had reminded her when they had woken in the bed they'd shared for the last few days. It was still early, as far as Ellen was concerned. In her time she would have been leaving to go to school now. She wouldn't have been up for several hours already, laying fires and preparing stuff. At least they had been able to eat before they left. Ellen had been eating the pottage which most working people lived on, without any fuss; it was mix of cereal and vegetables a bit like her usual breakfast of porridge. Apparently they were lucky because they also got to eat the family's leftovers; but not the trenchers that food was often served on during main meals. Those went to the poor. These last two days Ellen had learnt a lot!

Jayne didn't expect much in the way of answers. Ellen found she could nod here and there and Jayne would carry on. Walking allowed Ellen to think, though, and to worry. Worry about how she was going to get back, and how long she would have to manage here in this strange life. A little dog nipped past her legs and raced down to the edge of the stream, barking at the ducks had been waddling at the side of the water, forcing them to take flight for safety. Ellen couldn't help smiling at the familiarity of the sight. Some things didn't change.

Up ahead a crowd of people were gathering at the side of the pond. As the girls drew closer Ellen could see that they were watching something happening on the opposite bank. A woman screeched as she was pushed into a chair fixed to the end of a long arm that extended from a wooden contraption. As she was swung out over the pool, people shouted and jeered "Shoulda kept thee mouth shut, woman," and "thas a scold." Suddenly the arm dropped, plunging the woman into the water and keeping her under. Ellen held her breath. She could hardly believe what she was seeing. There was struggling, and splashing from the victim, and laughter from the watchers. Then, as the woman's efforts weakened, she was brought up, water streaming from her clothes, coughing and gasping. Ellen let out her own breath in relief.

"Jayne, what's"...but her question died away as the scold, who had almost recovered, started shouting back at the crowd, and was promptly dunked again.

Several of the crowd began to chant together

"She who shouts and rages more
Than ever did she do before,
Shall grace the stool, and have to take
A second turn into the lake,
No brawling wives, no furious wenches,

No fire so hot but water quenches."

Ellen stared at Jayne, kind Jayne, as she joined in the words. At her expression Jayne said "ye not heard tha' ballad? We had it from the ballad seller by the alehouse not a month ago."

After the third time under the water, the pathetic looking woman started crying "Let me go, let me go, by God's help I'll sin no more."

"She'll have to walk back 'ome all wet," Jayne said, with some satisfaction, taking Ellen's arm and turning away, the spectacle over. A game of bowls resumed on the green as Ellen struggled with the shock at Jayne's words. Men were hanging over a fence, and standing round in groups arguing about the match.

"There be Mr Bunnys, the landlord," Jayne noted, nodding to the man standing on the steps leading to what Ellen knew as the pub. "Betting and quaffing ale!" she snorted. "Tho' tis market day and folks be making the most of things now they're able."

"Weren't they always, then?" Ellen dared to ask. Jayne gave her a curious look.

"Twas the work of "Little Horn," the so called Lord Protector," she said, her lip curling. "Leastways, now he be gone dancing and music are allowed. Those that were for t'King's book of games were against the parliament, as ye must know."

"Yes, Cromwell was a puritan," Ellen thought, remembering her history, "but Charlie has been back on the throne for two years."

The market place was bustling, full of people. They stood aside to make way for a couple dressed in rich fabrics, and Ellen took the opportunity to take in as much as she could. The Guildhall was obvious, standing out from other buildings. So was the stone cross mounted on steps, which seemed to be watching over everyone. To the side of this was a man locked in the stocks. He was plastered with muck, his head hung down miserably. Several people aimed rotten fruit at him.

"What did he do?"

"He worra hooker, I hear tell."

Ellen was confused by her answer- hookers were women, weren't they?

"Hooking pays, I hear tell. He'll have caught a cloth or two out a window, and hawked it."

Some kind of material thief, then! Ellen would have asked more, but there were so much to see. The smell was strong, a mix of many not so clean bodies, animals, and over it all a strong whiff of fish. "Hmm, markets always smell of fish," Ellen thought, wrinkling her nose. She and Jayne walked slowly, weaving their way through the crowds.

The meat sellers were grouped in the Shambles. Several cheese stalls were set up, and there was fresh produce too. Ellen recognised carrots, beetroots, spinach, onions and radishes. There were dried beans and cereals; corn, wheat and oats that must have been stored over winter. Some stalls were a surprise, like the one selling tobacco and pipes, and the stationer's with its chapbooks, as well as quills and inks. Each stall displayed a sign showing their trade, "a bit like the signs pubs always have," she thought. There were women selling woollen garments, stockings like Jayne and most of the women wore. As they passed by Ellen heard some of the people nearby speaking a different language.

"That sounds like French," she said, unable to stop herself.

"Well, how wouldst thee know such a thing," Jayne said, surprised. "Tis, French indeed. Yon men are from the Calais Wool Guild. The Reverend has oftimes entertained some of them to dinner. He do speak French and Latin. He did "is learning at Cambridge. The University." she continued, with a note of pride. "He do have many books on his shelves... The Mistress can read, and so can Master James and Miss Katheryne."

Street sellers mingled with the crowds, some singing and calling, some selling or handing out leaflets. Jayne took one that was offered.

"I can read some," she said, peering at the crudely printed writing on the thin, rough paper. "And Miss Katheryne learned me to write my name."

Ellen looked over Jayne's shoulder at the paper. Although the writing looked different from what she was used to she could make out the words, and she read them slowly out loud.

"George Fox to speak at a Meeting to be held at the Manor House,"...Who's George Fox?"

Jayne turned her face, her eyebrows raised.

"He be the leader of that puritan lot they call Quakers now. Mr Bromskill holds meetings regularly at the house...how be it ye can read?"

"I learnt at school, of course," Ellen replied, distracted by discordant noises she was hearing over and above the babble of the market.

"School? Tis not for the likes of thee," Jayne retorted!

At that moment a throng of people broke through the crowd. They were banging pots and pans, shouting, leaping and sort of dancing. Many had instruments of sorts, and played them wildly with no tune or rhythm. In the middle of the pack was a mock horse, the rider wearing an ornate hat and a notice pinned to his front. People laughed and jeered, spurring the rabble on, but as they got closer some of the onlookers were whirled aside and pushed to the ground. People gathered outside the Guildhall had noticed. They were laughing and pointing and nudging with elbows to get the attention of their companions.

Just then a man and lady hurried through the Guildhall doors, the man red-faced with anger.

"Tis a charivaris with Lord Hastings at th'heart, and him watching!" Jayne gasped. "The daring! There's no-one likes the way business is done at t'mills on Soar. Tis oft unfair, so they tell, short measures or no good stuff given. Many try to go abroad, to Dishley, where folks reckon terms is fairer."

The rough music seemed at once to underline how mad her world had become. Not thinking, Ellen reached her long-hidden phone from her pocket. Holding it up to the preposterous sight, she pressed the camera button. A pinkish light enveloped her, and immediately everything seemed distant. She closed her eyes for a moment...

Stumbling backwards a step or two, Ellen opened her eyes. Stunned for an instant, she made a huge effort to regain her balance. She was back! Back in her bedroom, only it wasn't. Looking around her, Ellen could see it was just the same as last Saturday. Displays, staircase, everything the same.

"Ellen, come on, we're ready to move on."

Her parents were calling. It **was** last Saturday. Ellen smiled. She was really back! She pulled off the seventeenth century clothes and the headscarf she was wearing, flinging them into a corner. Straightening her long line shirt, Ellen ran downstairs.

Extract from a novel-in-progress, by the same name.

Debt to Karma
Stephen Ashurst

The sun streaked orange and red across a wide-open sky. A chill in the evening air gave a reminder that despite the warm day, summer hadn't arrived yet. The park bench at the top of Parliament Hill gave a spectacular view of the City Centre.

Gary shuddered at the cold and zipped up his lightweight jacket. A pang of sadness and fear bit into him as he knew this moment had to end soon. His unshaved face looked tired and the peppered grey stubble made him look older than he really was.

"Thank you for this," he said to the man sitting next to him. "I mean it, really."

The other man simply nodded. He wore a long, grey woollen coat, a grey flat cap and mirrored aviator shades that looked straight out of the 1980s. His face gave away no emotion or personality. Only that he was calm and composed; unnervingly so.

"It's beautiful isn't it?" said Gary. "I don't think I've been back here in a long time, not since..." The words stuck in his throat, choking him until he took a deep breath. He glanced awkwardly at his companion, then back at the vista.

"I didn't think I'd get to see it again, after you showed up. You know I can't pay the money back don't you?"

The man nodded gently.

"They know it too don't they? And that's why you're here."

Another awkward moment passed. Any conversation had been mostly one-sided.

"So what should I call you? Mr Kill?"

"If you like." The man replied softly.

"No I *don't* like. It makes me feel very uncomfortable. Frightened even. I appreciate the last request, this time you've allowed me, but not if I have to spend it in fear. Can I call you Mr Jones? I know it's not your name, at least I don't think it is. But it would make me feel better."

He shrugged. Gary took this to mean yes.

"This is where he died you know, my son, Charlie that is. We used to bring him here as a little boy to run around, ride his bike, all of that. He was a bright lad, good future. But he fell in with a bad crowd. They used to tease him and dare him to do stuff – which he always would. But he was never one of them, not properly." His lip trembled as he remembered. "There was a fight, apparently. They stabbed him in the neck and he died right here you know, on this bench. Those bastards!" He spat the last word through clenched teeth.

"Who did?" Mr Jones asked.

"This lot." Gary nodded to a gang of youths heading up the hill towards them. They were a little way off, but they were joking with each other and making noise. The tall one leading the way had a can of beer in his hand and a cigarette hanging out of his mouth. Another was lit by a smart phone pumping out some hip-hop music. Two others carried sports bags over their shoulders, also drinking. One of them gave a loud belch and threw his can over his shoulder. It made a quiet clatter as it rolled back down the pathway. They got louder as they came closer until they walked right up to the two of them. The tall one looked straight at them as if to question why they were sitting on his park bench. But he said nothing, simply spat on the floor in front of them and walked past. The rest of the gang glared at them as they passed by too. Eventually they decided to sit on the grass just a few feet behind the bench. The talking and laughing continued, but Gary had the feeling that some of it was being directed at him, although he couldn't tell for sure without turning to see, which he knew was bound to set them off.

Something hit the side of Gary's head; it glanced off and clattered on the bench next to him. It was an empty beer can. There were howls of laughter from behind him now.

"Excuse me." Gary said politely to Mr Jones. He got up and walked purposefully around the bench to the youths lounging on the grass. "You don't know me do you?" he asked.

"No mate, and we don't care. Piss off!" The tall one replied, lying flat on his back with his hands behind his head.

"Franco isn't it?"

"What's it to you, bitch?"

Gary took a couple of deep breaths, He looked down at this arrogant excuse of a human being. Someone who had wrenched all happiness from his life. "Charlie says hi," he replied finally. Pulling a kitchen knife out of his jacket pocket, he leapt onto the youth, aiming the knife for his chest. Franco twisted away just in time. The knife cut into the sleeve of his jacket and pinned him to the floor. Franco managed to push him off. One youth backed way in surprise, but the other two jumped onto Gary, pinning him face down on the ground and pulling his arms behind him. Franco pulled the knife from his coat and stood over his disarmed attacker.

"You just made a big mistake, bitch! Now I'm gonna cut you up."

"Don't do that please." Mr Jones spoke from the other side of the park bench.

"And who are you? His boyfriend?" Franco laughed.

"Shh." Mr Jones put his finger to his lips. "You two," he said pointing to the pair holding Gary down. "Stand up, I have an important job for you. I need you to help your friends back home. Do you understand?" The youth nearest stood and squared up to Mr Jones.

"Who are you to…"

"Do you understand?" he said much louder and with an unnerving menace in his voice.

"I hear you grandpa but you'll be…"

"Good" he said, then in a split second Mr Jones pulled a silenced pistol from his coat pocket and fired two shots. It sounded like two small sneezes but Franco dropped to ground screaming and clutching his knee. The fourth gang member, who had turned to run, also fell in the same way. "You two, remember what you need to do?" The two youths simply stared back at him in shock. "Do you want me to find someone to carry you as well?"

"No." The nearest one exclaimed meekly. "We'll do it. Don't shoot."

Franco was crying and swearing, dribble ran down his chin. Mr Jones knelt close to his face and pressed the gun barrel to his forehead.

"Shh, you're making too much noise."

Franco immediately bit his lip, letting only the quietest whimper escape. Mr Jones stood up and hid the gun back in his coat. The two able bodied youths helped their friends up as best they could. One of them reached out an arm to pick up the sports bags.

"Leave those please."

"No. You can't. That money is for…"

"I don't care. Leave it."

The two youths exchanged glances but obviously weren't going to challenge him. They turned and hobbled away as fast as they could.

"Thank you, you saved my life. I think." Gary struggled to his knees and was about to stand.

"Don't get up." Mr Jones walked behind him. Gary felt the gun barrel press against the back of his head.

"Of course. I spoke too soon didn't I? Forgot why we were here. So why did you bother saving me then?"

"The debt must be paid."

There was a click. Gary closed his eyes and waited for his execution. His heart raced. This was when your life was supposed to flash before your eyes, but it didn't. All he could think of was whether he would feel it. The pressure eased as the gun was removed. Gary still held his breath, waiting for something to happen. He opened one eye slowly, then the other. He couldn't hear anything. Very slowly he dared to turn his head. Expecting at any moment a flash and everything would be gone. But there wasn't one. The park behind him was empty. He spun round the other way. Still no-one. It was getting quite dark, but Gary could see clear enough that Mr Jones had gone. And so had the bags.

Spring Brake

Karen Ette

Tamsin watched Megan take a sip of frothy coffee.

"How are the evening classes going?" Megan asked, and wiped a creamy moustache from her top lip.

"Oh fine, I'm really enjoying them," Tamsin lied.

She met Megan's enquiring eyes over the rim of her own cup.

"And how is Aidan?"

"Oh, don't talk to me about him." Tamsin put her cup down, a little unsteadily, and she felt Megan's hand on her bare arm.

"What's he done this time, Tammy?" Megan was offering her a sympathetic smile, but Tamsin struggled to answer, her throat constricted and her eyes filled with tears. "He's hurt you so many times, please give him up," Megan said. Tamsin bit her lip and as the tears rolled down her cheeks she whispered "well, he's hurt me again, but not anymore, this is the last time."

"You've said that before."

"I mean it this time," Tamsin said softly and looked into Megan's wide, brown eyes.

"Tell me," Megan urged.

"You see this?" Tamsin pointed to her stomach, but didn't wait for an answer, "that's his child in there, but does he want to know? Oh no, says it can't be his, says I must have slept with someone else – not his responsibility!"

"And is it?"

"Of course it bloody well is. On my life, and my baby's." She patted her belly, "I have never slept with anyone else. It's his and he knows it."

"Have you had it out with him?"

"I've tried. I've even begged, but then this arrived." Tamsin threw a brown envelope onto the table between them. Megan picked it up and pulled out the letter Tamsin had received from a firm of solicitors. Tamsin watched Megan's face for a reaction, but it remained impassive as she read the legal jargon.

"This says you have to be out by the end of the month. Surely he doesn't need the flat; he has his own house hasn't he? I don't understand, how can he say you have to leave, especially as you are carrying his child?"

"Because it's his flat, and I haven't paid him any rent. He doesn't care about the baby either."

"What will you do?"

"Oh, I'll sort something out. I suppose I shall have to let him go."

"It's probably for the best," Megan said and pushed the letter back into the envelope.

Tamsin's tears had stopped and she felt her despair being replaced by harsh reality. "I expect he wants to move his new girlfriend in, which is why he wants me out."

"I suppose it would be good for you to make a clean break and move away."

"Oh, I'll make a clean break all right, don't you worry," Tamsin promised her friend.

*

Tamsin ripped the front page from her calendar to reveal an unsullied, new month. An early-morning beam of sunlight entered through the kitchen window; a sprinkling of motes danced in its path.

She opened her mobile phone for the hundredth time. Nothing. No texts, no emails, no missed calls. She checked the weather app. Normal for a spring day. She hadn't slept at all, but didn't feel tired. The cup of coffee she had made half an hour earlier was untouched, so she threw the cold liquid away and rinsed her cup. Leaning on the sink, she stared at the last dregs as they slid away and out of sight. The kitchen clock said ten to six; that gave her plenty of time to have a relaxing, hot bath before going to work and facing the day.

She took her time in getting ready and ensured that the persona she conveyed was one of innocence and confidence. She had to be extremely careful not to do anything unusual or out of routine. Every nerve in her body was taut with anxiety, but she needed to keep her head.

Tamsin arrived early and had time for a coffee before starting work. Sitting at her desk, she was still sipping the steaming liquid when Mike Taylor, the HR Manager and Megan's boss, appeared round the office door.

"Hey, Tam, I need a word with Aidan Massham, have you seen him today?"

She fought to keep her nerves in check, then smiled fixedly at him and said, "Who?" She shrugged. "I haven't seen anyone apart from you today, but then, I was in early; lots to do you know." Her relationship with Aidan had been a closely guarded secret, on his insistence, and now it suited her to disassociate herself from him.

"Be a love and ring his office would you, save me going back to mine?" Mike asked and winked.

"Yes, OK, just for you." She smiled at him and flicked through a list of telephone numbers, pretending she didn't know Aydan's extension, pleasantly surprised at how steady her hand was as she lifted the receiver and dialled. "No reply, sorry. I guess it's too early."

Mike shrugged and walked away, "Thanks anyway," he called over his shoulder as he disappeared down the corridor. Tamsin sighed and stared at the telephone; as she did so, the events of the night before replayed in her distracted mind.

She had parked her car two streets away from where Aidan lived and, keeping in the shadows and out of sight, walked to his house. It had been almost midnight; there were no lights on downstairs and a glow from a lamp had lit his bedroom window. She'd gasped on seeing his silhouette on the curtains, then a smaller figure had joined him. The two had embraced, passionately, before moving away. Shortly afterwards the light had been extinguished and the ferocity of her loathing had caused her to shake. His black car had been parked a few steps away on the road behind her. "How careless," she'd thought. Pulling her hood further over her face, she'd walked quietly over and pulled a pair of grips from her pocket and placed them against the shiny paintwork. Tempting though it had been to score an ugly scar over the bonnet, she'd resisted and instead lowered herself down until she had been able to squeeze underneath and between the two front wheels. The engine had been slightly warm, which for some inexplicable reason, had caused her anger to intensify and her determination to become absolute. She had easily found the steel brake-pipe to the nearside wheel. "Those evening classes had definitely paid off," she'd thought as she had placed the pair of grips on to the pipe. When she had squeezed hard she'd felt the pipe buckle and seal off the fluid. Satisfied with her work, she'd slid from under the car. Facing Aydan's house once more, she'd looked up at the bedroom window and brushed off her jeans.

"Goodbye Aidan," she'd whispered, and turned and walked away. A drift of daffodils by the roadside had rustled when she'd walked past them, as though they had been whispering gossip to each other.

Tamsin needed another coffee, so she typed a quick email to Megan in HR. *"Hi Megan, I'm on my way round, let's have coffee."* She pressed send, took a deep breath and headed off to see her friend. The lift was broken so she took the stairs to the fourth floor and on the way passed Computing Services where Aidan worked. There was a lot of activity and a dark-haired woman she didn't recognise rushed past in floods of tears. Tamsin carried on up the last flight of stairs, her legs felt unsteady and she noticed that her hands were shaking as she opened the door to the HR Office. Megan wasn't at her desk, and assuming that she had already set off for the canteen, Tamsin turned to leave, but Mike Taylor saw her and came from behind his desk; his face was almost grey and his usual cheerful air had vanished.

"I'm just going for a coffee with Megan," Tamsin told him.

"Sit down, Tamsin, I have some bad news." Mike's voice cracked as he spoke. Tamsin was glad to sit down; she could feel panic beginning to rise within her and her wide eyes rested on Mike's solemn face. "It's a very sad day for this company. You couldn't get hold of Aidan Massham for me this morning because he crashed his car on the way in this morning." Tamsin struggled to keep her face impassive. She swallowed a couple of times before trusting herself to speak.

"I'm sorry, how awful, I'm afraid I don't know him," she lied, "is he all right?"

"Apparently his car swung into a line of traffic," Mike continued.

"So," she thought, "my theory was right; squashing the nearside brake-pipe caused the car to swing into the oncoming traffic when he'd braked."

"He's on life support, if he does pull through he may have brain damage."

She almost felt relieved that he hadn't been killed, even thought she had felt like killing him, but she would never have been able to live with his death on her conscience, even if he had cruelly used her, hurt her and cast her aside.

"Tamsin," Mike's voice cut into her pre-occupation, "Tamsin, that's not all." She looked at Mike and his words became distant and hollow as her world swirled around her and she slipped into unconsciousness as she heard him say:

"I'm afraid Megan was in the car with him, I'm so sorry, she didn't make it."

No Ball Games
Donna Shepherd

As Florence Carter parked next to a large camouflaged Army truck, she glanced out at the ugly brick and concrete building that loomed over the car park of the military base. In what she believed could only have been an attempt to mask the inhospitable building, baskets and tubs of brightly coloured spring flowers surrounded the "Reception" sign.

"Are they all soldiers?" Carter asked the man sitting next to her, turning the car engine off and indicating the large group of people standing at the opposite side of the car park.

"Yes," Sergeant Phillips replied sharply, "they are all squaddies, and better at what they do than any police bod you've ever worked with."

Darren Miller coughed. "So how is it that you left the Army to join our miserable profession then, Sarge?" he asked, winking at Carter in the rear view mirror.

"It was time for a change," he said abruptly before turning to face Carter. "Just don't let me down," he hissed at her, "this lot know the real meaning of having balls, so here is your chance to prove you deserve that place on the team!"

Carter tightened her grip on the steering wheel, imagining the look on Phillips face as she repeatedly slammed his head in the car door. Reasoning, arguing, even shouting at this man got her no-where and she had learned to keep her mouth tightly closed.

"You will not show me up in front of Axel," he said, indicating the man who had left the group and was walking towards them. "Remember, Carter, there's a lot of money on this bet, so it's time to man up and grow that pair that you keep reassuring me you have!" Hesitating as he got out of the car, Phillips murmured "plus it's about time I got one over on the old bastard." Slamming the car door shut, he strode over to greet the man approaching him.

"Remind me again, Daz, what am I doing here on a day off at eleven a.m.?" Carter asked. "Good grief, I should still be lazing around on the sofa, my purring cat next to me and a huge mug of coffee in my hand. Instead," she continued, "I'm here, having to listen to his macho bullshit.

Daz laughed. "Come on lady, you being the fittest bird on the force was eventually going to get you into bother. The Sarge may be a misogynist arsehole, but even he can't ignore how hard you train." Leaning forward, Daz placed a hand on her shoulder. "We know he has a betting problem," he said, "but he can't do anything to you if you lose – you know that right?"

Carter nodded.

"I've told you before, it's not you. He's a relic and has made it perfectly clear that you belong at home, preferably pregnant, and in the kitchen!" Daz chuckled. "The fact that he has made no effort to get to know you, while ignoring the common opinion that you're great at what we do, enables me to say bollocks to him!"

Carter laughed. "I know you're right," she said, "but I have never come across anyone like him before. His attitude to women would be laughable if it wasn't so serious. I'm a police officer for god's sake, I do not need to "grow a pair", as he so delicately puts it – they let me carry a gun, but oh no, that's just not good enough for him!"

Taking a deep breath, Carter opened the door of the car and got out. Despite being cold, the sun was shining and there was the definite promise of summer in the air. From the opposite side of the car park came the hum of voices and laughter.

"Don't let Phillips bully you Flo," Darren Miller warned as he joined her. "You know these ex-military men sometimes have issues. Just get yourself round the course and try to enjoy it. I'll follow behind and make sure there's no funny business."

"Ha, she actually looks nice," Carter said, gesturing at her opponent who was standing with her colleagues. "Wonder why she agreed to this?" she mused. "It's on the barracks and I bet the poor cow has to train here daily."

*

Carter shifted her right leg a quarter of an inch on the narrow foothold and couldn't resist a painful whimper as her calf muscle screamed in protest. Giving into temptation she gazed upwards at the expanse of wall towering above her. She instantly regretted it; it felt like she hadn't moved at all and was only a third of the way up the sodding thing. Defeat seemed imminent and she hated the idea of it; she never failed. Here she was, stuck on a bloody twelve-foot wall in the middle of March just because of a pointless bet, a bet that she wasn't even getting a pay-out from.

Carter thought of the taunts from her colleagues and the anger from the Sarge. No other woman in the force could match her and doing a circuit of the assault course against a squaddie should have been a bit of fun, even a laugh. Now it just seemed like a waste of a day off.

"You need a hand?" said a voice from above her. Carter looked up to see Private Blake, her opponent, sitting on top of the wall.

"Christ! How long have you been sat there?" Carter asked, followed by a muttered "and more importantly how the hell did you get up there?"

Blake chuckled, a surprisingly friendly sound.

"I've been running this assault course forever," she answered. "In the early years they'd make us run round it daily and finding ways to avoid the pain was the only way through it."

From her hanging position Carter could see the logic of this; she too would need some way to make the pain less so. Her muscles were screaming, but the thought of losing face kept her fingers tight.

"Just to your left is a ledge," Blake said. "It's not obvious but it is there, feel with your feet."

Carter pulled her legs up slightly and sure enough there was a ledge.

"How come I couldn't see that from the ground?" she asked.

"Your brain is all out trying to simply get you round the course," Blake replied, "more often than not it clouds your rationale and stops you seeing things."

Now that Carter had her feet on solid wood she could loosen her grasp. Taking a deep breath she bent as low as she dared and thrust her body upwards, feeling hands on her upper arms as she did so. Blake had grabbed her and was helping her to the top. This was surely not part of the plan, but Carter was too knackered to care. "Thanks," she gasped as she swung her leg over the top. "That was way harder than I imagined. I thought this was a team-building exercise, with a spot of competitiveness thrown in. I didn't expect it to be so tough."

Blake laughed again. "Do you know nothing about army men?" she asked. "It's all about the bet and life on base can get really tedious!" She sighed. "Time off is rare so entertainment is key, and sadly for me, that revolves around stupid bets and way too much television."

Carter grinned, her breathing had returned to normal and she was beginning to like this girl more and more.

"Come on," Blake said, "we are better than this shit. How do you feel about sticking it to them and walking over that line together?"

"That's a deal," Carter said as both women jumped onto the raised platform on the other side of the wall and fell into step beside each other. The air was sweet after the earlier rain and Carter inhaled deeply, feeling the stress of the morning's challenge slide away.

"What would you normally be doing today?" Blake asked.

"It's my day off, first of three and would involve the gym followed by a seriously lazy afternoon on the sofa with my cat, Tom."

Blake chuckled, "Great name, how old is he?"

"The vet thinks he's about seven," she replied. "A man brought a bag into the front office at the nick and I just happened to be in there. The top of the bag fell sideways and this gorgeous, large white-and-tabby head peeked out. He has the most amazing green eyes." Carter looked at the floor, "Ha, listen to me going on," she said. "I don't usually get to talk about my wonderful cat, but I have to confess, I was hooked," she admitted, "right there and then. It's the closest I've ever come to falling in love."

Both women laughed.

"He sounds wonderful" Blake said. "How long ago was that?"

"Four years ago and I can honestly say he is the only serious relationship I've ever had," she answered. "So what about you," Carter asked, "what would your day off involve?"

"Ah, I'd be here, rarely get off the base but there is loads to do, so it's not all bad and I have no excuse to not go to the gym as it's in the next block from mine."

Carter stopped and looked at Blake, an expression of incredulity on her face. "You rarely leave the base? Why, when Birmingham is so damn near?"

Blake sighed. "I haven't been shopping in a long time and can only imagine the blokes' faces if I suggested a shopping trip! My parents live in Scotland," Blake continued, "they moved when I joined the Army. Dad's parents retired up there and Mom's died years ago so they decided it was the perfect time. I can get to them in four hours and it's a lovely drive. Mom and I tend to hit the shops then, she hates my grunge look!"

Carter grinned. "It looks like I found you in the nick of time then. How about we kick this friendship off with a drink in The Arms later?"

"Oh!" said Blake, her eyes widening in mock exhilaration, "a drink in a pub with a girl. Maybe we can have a real conversation, talking about something other than football, rugby and breasts!"

"Ha-ha, can't promise anything more than a beer. I only ever socialise with blokes too, but I do promise to not talk about breasts!" Carter replied.

Carter looked at Blake while they walked. It was hard to believe that the woman next to her was so friendly and relaxed. She had always supposed that women in the army had to be butch and aggressive, but Blake was only slightly taller than Carter's five foot eight, and her hair was long and dark, tied back in an elaborate knot.

Carter stopped and turned round. Something moved in the undergrowth, about a hundred yards behind them. She smiled and lifted her arm in greeting as a man stepped onto the path and waved at them.

"You ok, Hun?" he called as he walked towards them.

Carter nodded, "I'm fine, Daz." Turning to Blake she asked, "What's your first name?"

"Caitlin," Blake replied.

"Daz Miller, Caitlin Blake," Carter introduced the two as they shook hands. "Mate from work and my own personal bodyguard," she teased, as he punched her lightly on the arm.

"We won't be long," she said, then added, "we're taking the scenic route, a bit of girl time."

Daz hooted. "Sarge Phillips is doing his nut," he said, "that information will send him completely over the edge." Daz turned and started to walk away. "I thought you'd had an accident," he called over his shoulder, "but I should have known better."

Carter looked at Blake who had raised her eyebrow in query. "Yum," Blake said, "and to think I thought army lads held the monopoly on bodies like that!"

Carter smiled. "Yeah, he's worked hard to look like that. Daz joined the unit a couple of years ago and if we are not working you'll find him in the gym. He's a genuine bloke which is a rarity in my experience."

"Sounds like you have a soft spot for him," Carter observed. "Any romance with that one?" she asked.

"Ha no, nothing like that," Carter replied, before adding seriously, "but he is my friend and I would trust him with my life."

Blake nodded. "A rarity indeed," she said. "Anyway, what's the deal with your Sarge?" she asked. "He sounds like a right tool."

Carter grimaced, "I wish I knew," she replied, "he transferred from another force a few months ago and well…," pausing, she glanced at Blake, "I hate to play the, "it's because I'm a woman card," but it genuinely is because of that."

"What? Seriously?"

Carter took a deep breath and stopped walking. She glanced around and then went and sat on a log at the side of the path. "Every job, every call," she said, "it's like he's watching, waiting for me to cock it all up." She turned to look at Blake who had sat down next to her. "I know that being an armed cop is not an everyday job for most people but it's like he doesn't trust me…" she paused, "he even made me clean and disable my gun last week in front of him – just so he could check that I knew what I was doing!" Carter rolled her shoulders in frustration. "The lads were great when I joined the unit," she continued, "accepted me, and knew the hoops I'd jumped through to get a place on the team. Being a woman, well it just didn't matter to them. But this Sarge visibly bristles when I book on duty."

Blake reached out and patted Carter's arm. "Some men," Blake said, "and I do speak from experience here, find women, well.... intimidating, threatening and owing to their own personal issues, dominant father, controlled mother and sisters, blah, blah, blah, they are incapable of allowing you to just be. To them, you belong in a certain kind of domestic-sphere box and they struggle to accept what it is you do." Blake let out a long breath. "Of course, I may be wrong. I've only set eyes on the bloke but if what you say is true, then his issue is nothing to do with you. Have you thought about reporting his behaviour?"

"Not yet," Carter replied. "I have started to log comments that he makes and I don't want to let the prick get to me, but work just isn't the same since he arrived. Ideally, I'd hoped that by working with him he would see that he had nothing to criticise, but it hasn't worked out that way. I'm good at my job, very good at my job," Carter sighed in exasperation. "The job is hard enough without the atmosphere that he creates within the nick. He's rude to me in front of the others and always dismisses anything I say. He's the stereotypical alpha male," she continued, "he never misses an opportunity to make a lewd comment regarding women and he seems to live at the betting shop. In fact, this whole day has been about him and his stupid bets."

Carter stood up and stretched her arms above her head. "Come on," she said, "that drink is calling – let's get back!"

"What's your first name?" Blake asked as they started walking.

Carter took a breath. "Florence," she said, "and no, you can't call me Flo!"

*

Sergeant Phillips stood rigid with anger. "You stupid cow! What the hell where you thinking? You are by far the fittest and you let the bitch talk you into....."

"With respect, sir," Carter interrupted, "it was a pointless exercise and I wasn't going to risk injury for a stupid bet." Carter held his glare, returning it with her own no-nonsense expression.

"I won't forget this Carter," he growled as he walked away.

What a prick, Carter thought to herself. Mind you, she reasoned, it had got her a decent work out and she had made a new ally.

Carter glanced over to where Blake was standing, surrounded by her colleagues. No-one was yelling at her, disappointed in her performance.

*

Carter sipped her coffee as she waited for the shift briefing to begin. Two weeks had passed since her day on the assault course, but Phillips had continued to criticise and belittle her. She watched him as he entered the room, all fake smiles and masculine bullshit. He'd earned the nickname "slippers" soon after joining the shift eighteen months ago as he refused to leave the station unless absolutely necessary. God alone knew what he did, but he could always be found in the Sergeants office, shuffling pieces of paper in an attempt to appear busy.

Today however, was different. Unbelievably, he had deigned to leave the safety of the nick, deciding that she was to spend the shift with him. It seemed that this was an added level to her punishment, as so far, he had not missed an opportunity to verbalise how worthless she was to the shift, as a woman.

"Balls, is what you need in this job, Carter," Phillips droned at her as she drove out of the police station yard. "It takes a special kind of man to do the job we do. Solid balls of steel that make those tough decisions, decisions no woman should ever have to face, easy for us blokes to make."

Him and his sodding balls, Carter thought, the same bloody mindless drivel, spouted with the same irritating lofty tone. In an attempt to block out his nonsense, she focused her attention on the cars in front of her. The shift would pass slowly unless she found something interesting to stop.

After a while, Phillips ceased talking and the car was filled with an oppressive silence.

"Reports of shouting and screaming from the vicinity of 122 Radgate Street," the controller's voice said, shattering the agonising silence. "Romeo delta two one, can you attend?" he asked.

"Romeo delta two one," Carter replied, "Yes, two minutes away and on route." Finally, she thought, pressing the relevant emergency response buttons on the dashboard, something to alleviate the boredom.

*

The police car's engine changed pitch as Carter bought the vehicle to a halt.

Unlocking her seatbelt, Carter peered out of the window. "God this estate depresses me," she said staring at the pallid grey of the council houses, which were clustered round a small patch of grass. There was a lone daffodil swaying in the breeze, it's bright yellow colour defiant against a group of surly-faced teenagers that were standing near the "no ball games" sign, smoking and kicking a ball around.

"I'd resort to habitual violence if I was forced to live here," Carter said as she climbed out of the car. "I'm guessing that's the informant," indicating a woman who was waving at them from the pavement.

"I'll deal with this Carter," Phillips said pompously. "You go and talk to that woman and I'll meet you back at the car. I'm sure it's nothing serious and always better coming from a man who knows what he's doing."

Suppressing her irritation, and mentally flicking him the finger, Carter locked the police vehicle and walked across the road to join the kindly-faced woman.

*

"Bye, Mrs Harper, and thanks again for the tea and cake," Carter called, closing the door behind her and making her way back to the car. There was no sign of Phillips and checking her watch, Carter was amazed to see that thirty minutes had passed since she'd left him at the car.

"Bloody man has probably bored the pants off them by now," she muttered to herself, walking through the dilapidated gate of number twenty-two.

A gunshot shattered the silence. "You don't know anything," a man's voice screamed from inside.

Ducking down, Carter inched her way around the side of the house, pressing the emergency response button on her radio set. Heart pounding, she unclipped the catch on her gun holster and cautiously peered through a rip in the net curtain, which was draped across the window.

Sergeant Phillips sat at the kitchen table with his hands bound in front of him, blood running from his nose. His eyes were wide open with fear and he was staring at someone that Carter couldn't see.

"Come on, you bastard," she whispered to herself, "show me where you are – let's see that face."

Carter removed her gun and looked around her for a safe entry point into the house. As she began to move along the back wall towards the door, Carter was startled by the sound of crying coming from the wooden shed that had been roughly attached to the building.

"Please help me," a female voice sobbed from inside.

Taking a deep breath to steady the hand holding her gun, Carter approached the shed and opened it. Lying on the floor was a blonde woman whose hands and feet were tied. Her face was streaked with blood and tears, her limbs covered in bruises and her dress ripped and filthy.

"It's ok," Carter whispered to the woman, as she knelt on the floor and deftly removed her penknife from her utility belt, cutting the rope that was tied around the woman's hands and feet. "It's all going to be ok. What's your name?" she asked.

"Helen," the woman replied pulling herself into a sitting position and rubbing her ankles and wrists, "please help me, don't leave me here."

"I won't, but I have to help my colleague. Can you tell me what happened and do you know how many people are in the house?"

"Just Jay," Helen stammered. "He let me out of here this morning and took me into the house. I thought he was going to let me eat, maybe take a shower, but he jumped at me – you know?" Carter nodded. "Well," Helen continued, "I couldn't face that, not again. So I started screaming, hoping someone would hear." Helen took a deep breath and wiped her arms across her nose. "He attacked me and threw me in here. I heard the doorbell and more muffled sounds before that gunshot. Oh God, do you reckon he's killed your mate?"

"No, he's ok, I saw him through the window. Look I have to go now, Helen, but a colleague will be here very soon. Stay still and quiet please. You're safe now," Carter said stepping back out of the shed, and walking towards the house. She pushed the back door and let it swing open, carefully surveying the room for anything that could be used against her. As satisfied as possible that there was no-one lurking in wait for her, Carter stepped into the house.

Moving silently, she crossed the hallway and stopped outside the kitchen door. There were no sign of Jay and no noise from within the room. Crouching low, Carter looked through the open door and met the frightened gaze of Phillips who flicked his head to the door behind him, indicating that Jay had left the room. Putting her finger to her lips, Carter signalled for him to fall off his chair.

Gun extended, Carter inched her way into the room as Phillips threw himself sideways onto the floor.

The crash brought Jay running back into the room, right arm at ninety degrees, gun pointing at the ceiling. "What the fu....." he shouted before screaming in fright at the sight of Carter.

"Stand still," she shouted, "I'm an armed police officer."

Jay lowered the gun towards Phillips, and instinctively Carter fired two rounds at his chest and one at his face.

Carter walked over to Phillips who was sitting on the kerb, head in hands.

Hunkering down next to him she patted him awkwardly on the shoulder.

"Alright, Sarge?" she asked.

Phillips glanced sideways at her.

"Nice job, Carter," he said, as he stood up to go with the paramedic who had arrived. Looking back over his shoulder at her, Phillips grinned, "that took balls, lady," he said. "Thank you!"

Extract from a novel-in-progress

Bluebell Woods
Melinda Ingram

Jack leant against the young oak tree, his legs stretched in front of him, ankles crossed. Under his helmet, with its camouflage pattern in sandy greys, his eyes closed for a few moments. His face turned up towards the early morning sun filtering through the newish, shiny green leaves. His hands held his gun, at rest, on the remnants of his combat trousers. He sighed. It was so peaceful here. No wailing sirens warning of incoming rockets, no rat-a-tat from gunfire. And it was green, so green, not the dry, dusty yellow he'd begun to hate.

This tree, **his** tree, was only five years old, but with a trunk of about six inches and a height of about six foot it made a great resting place. It was his place now, or one of his places. There was a little bit of him in special spots near the seaside, in the country, and in town. He alternated between each place, but this was probably his favourite, especially in spring.

Opening his eyes just a little, Jack smiled at the gently waving carpet of bluebells, which surrounded him, interspersed with patches of new grass. The flowers covered the ground under all the recently planted trees and stretched deep into the established wood beyond the nearby path. In the summer his beach took up much of his attention. He also had important work to do at the two memorials he visited in July and November, where he knew he would see his folks. This, though, was the time when he was most needed here. People came for the beauty of the woods, the spring flowers, the wildlife. They came for walks, to exercise, to picnic. And sometimes they came to make mischief. Sounds of children calling to each other reached his ears. He smiled as a fluffy grey collie loped towards him and sniffed his boots.

"Hey, doggy." He reached out to stroke the animal, but it stared, lifted one side of its lip, and backed away, barking. Jack shrugged. He got to his feet, ready to patrol.

*

You can leave each other alone, now – we're here," Rob directed to the back seat of the car, as he pulled into a space in the Outwoods car park.

"Yay, we're here!" Jay echoed, his nose pressed to the glass as Emmy leaned over for a better view.

"We will see the bluebells, won't we, Dad?

"We're visiting your sister, you know, but yes, we will see the bluebells, hopefully masses of them."

"Okay, everyone out. Boots on. It'll be muddy up there after all the rain we've had," Anna told them as she opened the rear door.

"Release the hounds, darling," she continued needlessly, as Rob was already lifting the back, leads at hand. Two border collies, one black and white, the other a mix of mottled greys, leapt out.

"Maddie, you're a good girl," he told the black and white dog who sat waiting at his feet. "And you're a mutt!" The grey dog spun in circles, yapping as Rob tried to fix the lead to her collar.

"Can I hold Shady?" asked Emmy, as she finished pulling on her pink wellies, throwing her shoes into the back of the car.

"In a bit," came the answer. "She's too excited just now. On the way back, when they've had a good run."

Emmy made a pout, and turned on her heels to run after Jay, who was already some way up the path to the woods.

"I love it here." Anna smiled up at Rob, as she linked her dog-free arm through his. "I'm so glad we heard about the tree planting on Radio Leicester."

It was still quite early for a Sunday. Dew sparkled in the grass on either side of the path. The gravel was wet, and where it had worn away their boots sucked slightly as they walked. Nearer the woods and away from cars, Rob leaned down and unclipped the dog leads. Both animals raced off after the children. Sunlight trickled through the trees, pooling in patches on the forest floor. There was a smell of damp wood mixed with the scent of spring flowers. Continuous rippling birdsong was punctuated with laughter and yipping.

Rob watched, as the children and dogs ran ahead. He patted Anna's arm with his free hand. "They're happy. And I'm sure Meggie is too. We did the right thing bringing her here. She loved bluebells."

"There's some!" Anna pointed off to the side of the path. A few bluebells were scattered sparsely here and there amongst the woody debris.

Emmy and Jay came running back towards their parents, the dogs leaping up and round them.

"Mum, Dad, come and look," Emma called.

"We've got something to show you," Jay added, panting.

The children grabbed their parents" hands and pulled them.

"OK, we're coming, we're coming."

Around the corner all four stopped. Emmy and Jay watched for their parents" reactions.

"Oh, Rob, how beautiful," Anna sighed. A sea of bluebells covered the ground as far as they could see, a light breeze wafting the blue and green gently, so that waves rippled in the dappled sunlight. It was perfect.

Not long afterwards they reached the tree that they had planted on that day five years ago, Anna heavily pregnant, and Rob with Emmy on his back. It was an oak, like the other young trees in this area of the wood. They stood for a moment, then all caught hands and circled the tree, as the dogs weaved in between them, and then flopped to the ground.

"Hello, Meggie! We've all come to tell you how much we love you, darling!" Anna said. "You'd be nine now, big sister to Jay and Emmy."

"Bluebells are blue, dilly, dilly,

Bluebells are green," Jay sang

"That's Lavender, silly." Emmy protested, gripping his arm

"When I am king, dilly, dilly,

You shall be queen." Jay persisted, twisting away from his sister.

"I've brought you a heart stone I found on holiday," Emmy said, addressing the tree seriously. Taking a beach pebble from her pocket, she pressed it into the ground at the base of the trunk.

"That was really nice, both of you," praised Rob. "Meggie, you'll always be with us." He bent and firmed the soil round the base of the young oak.

"I found a poem by a lady called Elizabeth Mason on the internet, Meggie. I thought you'd like it," Anna pulled the typewritten paper from her pocket and read:

"Come walk with me through bluebell woods,
And see the proof of God's sweet love.
Long rays of sunlight trickling down,
Among the trees in search of ground.
A piece of heaven here below,
Creation at its best on show.
Echoes of a distant thrush,
We know that He is here with us."

They stood quietly for a moment, listening to the blackbirds, and rustling leaves.

Voices in the distance.

Voices getting louder.

"Hey you nerds," came a shout. "Whoo, hugging a tree."

"Tree-huggers! Oh no, there's four of them." Screams of laughter followed.

Three lads on bikes had ridden up towards them. One pulled his bike into a wheelie and crashed it off the forest track into the mass of bluebells. The others followed his lead. They seemed to be taking delight in crushing as many of the flowers as they could, standing up on their pedals, and whooping as they spun their bikes on the back tyres.

"Hey, what do you think you're doing?" Rob shouted at them, starting forward.

"Leave them, Rob." Anna pulled at Rob's arm. "Leave them. We'll call the Park Rangers. The number's on the gate. Let's get the dogs and go".

As they clipped on the dogs' leads the sunlight seemed to switch off. The woods went quiet as birdsong stilled. Rob and Anna guided the children away from the altercation, back towards the way they'd come. A cold draught took them by surprise, and all four turned. However, the main force of the blast was not for them. It whirled up the three delinquents and their bikes, holding them suspended high in the air. Their whoops changed to screams.

Rob and Anna held their breath, and caught hands, holding a child each in close to their bodies. Both dogs cowered on the ground, whining. After what seemed like forever, the wind suddenly stopped. Youths and bikes crashed to the ground. There was a long pause, where nothing happened except moaning. Even the dogs went quiet. Gradually, all three hooligans managed to extricate themselves from the heap of bike parts and limbs, struggling to stand.

"M....F...er! My bike's mangled, man!"

"My Dad's gonna go mental!"

The third boy sank back to the ground, sniffing, and wiping his eyes with his sleeve.

Maddie and Shady got to their feet, both of them barking with high pitched yelps.

"What just happened, Daddy?" Emmy asked.

"I don't know, Poppet, perhaps the ghosties got them. I think they might have learnt their lesson," Rob answered, still dealing with his own shock.

"Don't say things like that to them, Rob," admonished Anna.

Rob pulled at the dogs" leads. "Shut-up the pair of you," he told the still barking dogs. "Come on, time for Sunday lunch. We'll open a bottle of wine. I don't know about you, Anna, love, but I need a drink."

*

"Rest in Peace" they told him, everyone who came to visit. And Jack did, most of the time, but it wasn't always easy. There were all sorts here, with trees of their own; a couple of babies, kids, but mostly oldies. Some could move, like him, but mostly they stayed put. No, it wasn't them that kept Jack vigilant. It was his purpose – his job was to look after his surroundings, to guard them from those who wanted to make trouble, to defile or destroy. He was a protector.

Jack stood and watched as a family approached, man and woman arm in arm, two kids running a little ahead. They were OK. He watched, with tears in his eyes, as Meggie listened to their words and reached for the heart stone. It was very like the messages his family brought to him on his special days, when he, too, wanted to reach out and touch his loved ones. Meggie smiled through the tears running down her blotchy face, still marred by the meningitis that had robbed her of life. Then her eyes widened and her mouth came open with horror as they first heard, and then caught sight of the carnage that had begun.

Jack stretched out his hand and drew Meggie to him, as her family turned to leave. She put her arms round his legs and buried her head into his thigh. Jack swallowed, and fought to control the rage that was building. He was a professional. Still, he felt the hair under the back of his helmet prickle, his mouth felt dry and his breathing shortened.

It was time for action!

Laid at my Feet
Stephen Ashurst

He staggered down the busy city street, late in the afternoon on this cold and damp day. It was starting to get noticeably brighter at this time of year, but it was still bloody cold. He seemed to be bumping shoulders with more pedestrians than seemed possible. Were they aiming for him? It didn't matter, they didn't matter. His smart grey suit was looking less so – now that he'd been wearing it for three days straight.

"What are *you* staring at?" He shouted at a little girl holding her mother's hand. She looked worried and her mother quickly hugged her close before glaring back at him. "And you?" He yelled at her too. Served her right, why was everyone heading the wrong way today? He turned and stared after the woman, what right did she have to judge him anyway? He spat on the floor then set off again, only to walk into a tall man in a suit and long woollen coat. It almost knocked him off his feet, but the man just walked on regardless. "Well excuse me!" He shouted, arms in the air. "Anyone else want to take a pop?"

"Fresh spring flowers?" A frail voice spoke from the ground nearby.

"What?"

"Fresh flowers, young man? The herald of spring time." An elderly squat woman knelt on an old worn-out blanket on the pavement. She gave him a warm and toothless smile, then held out a small bunch of brightly coloured flowers. They were wrapped in dirty, torn cellophane and brown paper, but somehow looked bright and healthy. "For a young lady perhaps?"

"Why in God's name would I part with hard-earned cash for your bedraggled weeds? I have more important things to worry about. My life is in danger!"

"These flowers are beautiful and full of life, but I wouldn't expect you to understand that," she said sadly and took the flowers away. "You are lost."

"Oh really?"

"I know your type." She sighed.

"I seriously doubt it. Look at this." He held up his right hand, bandaged tightly but blood had soaked through in several places, running onto the cuff of his shirtsleeve and suit. "This is what they did as a warning. They cut off my little finger!"

"Maybe you shouldn't spend time with them," she said without even looking up.

"Not that easy is it? Not now that I owe them money."

"Then pay them."

"Yeah, three hundred thousand is not so easy to get from my piggy bank."

"Then sit down and tell me about it." She patted the bit of blanket next to her.

"What? I'm not going to sit with you, you smell of cat food and sick."

"Suit yourself. Have a nice life, whatever's left of it."

He clutched his hand then turned and kicked the wall repeatedly. "Shit, shit, shit! What am I going to do? There's nothing I can do!" He said tugging at his hair.

"Run away then." The old woman suggested, carefully arranging another small bouquet of bright but shabbily wrapped flowers, picked from the battered cardboard box next to her.

He frowned in concentration, then stared off into the distance. "I wouldn't get far, I've got no money. No enough anyway." He knelt down and grabbed her arm. "Have you got some? I need two, maybe three hundred. That should see me for a couple of days."

"Ha! If I had that kind of money, do you think I would be here?" She laughed and pulled her arm free.

"Shit." He slumped down next to her. "Then I'm dead."

"Maybe."

He turned and stared at her, hoping against all probability that she had an answer. "What do you mean maybe? Oh wait I could hide out couldn't I? Perhaps live here on the street. Maybe not here exactly, it's a bit too obvious, but near the bus station there's people on the back streets."

"You wouldn't last five minutes, if you don't mind my saying."

"Why not? You don't think I could hack it?"

"It's because *you* don't live there," she said grabbing his shoulder this time. "You're still living in your world of money, cars, houses and fast food. A plastic card can give you everything you need, you've no idea what it really feels like to be poor and alone, rejected by society. I'm not allowed into your world. When I'm cold and hungry I can't just call by the take-away for a freshly cooked meal then curl up to sleep in a warm bed. I eat whatever scraps I can find and when I go to sleep on a cold doorstep, I just pray I won't be stabbed in the night for my blanket. So tell me, why should you be allowed into my world as a tourist? Staying just as long as it suits before leaving all of us to pick up your cosy life again."

"What did you mean just then, when you said maybe? What other options are there?"

"You could change."

"Ha, it's a bit late for that, Grandma, I'm in way too deep." He folded his arms and looked away.

"Then you can face what's coming to you." She gave him a shove, practically knocking him over. "Move, you're putting off potential customers," said the old woman.

"OK, well maybe I can change a bit if you can hide me for a day or two. At least until I figure out what to do." He seemed oblivious to her attempts to move him and just carried on talking.

"Then it's a deal, let's shake on it." The old woman held out a dirty, gnarled little hand, which he took willingly. But she clutched his good hand with such force and strength that he felt his knuckles crack and his muscles ache. He tried to pull free but her grip was too strong. "Now it's time for you to change from your selfish, self-absorbed world and start a new life. You will grow and rise up from the dirt of the ground to be a better person, leaving behind possessions, money and material objects that cause nothing but misery and suffering. Instead you will embrace a self-less life, ascending towards the light and blossom into a good soul with a kind heart." She released her grip and let him sit back, clutching his painful hand.

"Wow, that really hurt!" He stared in amazement at the smiling face in front of him, but her outline had begun to soften and he was feeling light headed. "I'm just going to stay here on the floor for a minute or two."

"Don't worry, it's the start of your change." She held his shoulder to steady him. "Here, why not take a moment to look through these flowers, enjoy their beauty and forget about your old problems, they don't exist any more."

"OK." He let out a big sigh. The thought of being caught now seemed trivial, unimportant to him. As if it were someone else's problem. "There are so many colours here," he said examining the flowers in the box. "They look so fresh and alive."

There were daffodils and tulips amongst all kinds of flowers. He had no idea what many of them were. They were all beautiful and strong but he still handled them with care to make sure he didn't damage any. How did she manage to get all of these? She wouldn't have the money to buy them, assuming they weren't stolen someone must have given them to her. Perhaps she did steal them, but that didn't seem right. Something told him these represented good and that they could only bring happiness to people who saw them. They made him look at the world in a positive light. Sure there was death and killing, that didn't disappear, but there was so much love and life to be had. This was a time to reach for the light and make the most of being alive.

"Where did you get these? If you don't mind me asking." He asked, but there was no response. He looked up to see he was alone on the old blanket with nothing but the box of flowers. "Hello?" He realised he didn't know anything about the old woman, not even her name.

He barely had time to get used to this realisation before he was yanked by the arms up from the ground and held by two large men. A third smaller man, immaculately dressed in a black shirt and trousers, was staring at him. He recognised the scarred and shaved head, and the mouth full of gold teeth, as belonging to the one person in this world he really wanted to avoid. Known to all simply as 'the Manager'.

"You." The man stated firmly, grabbing his jaw and holding up a photograph. "Have you seen this face?"

He was staring a picture of himself, a surveillance photo by the looks of it, sitting drinking a coffee in the park. Must have been when he was meeting one of his contacts. Judging by the coat he was wearing it could only have been taken within the last six months.

"I, I..." He didn't know what to say. How could he not tell it was him?

"Speak! Or perhaps I need to liberate one of your fingers." The Manager nodded to the man holding his right arm, who immediately grabbed a hand and held it forward. The bandage was gone and amazingly all his fingers were intact.

"What? How?" He spluttered.

"You're not making any sense, too much cheap vodka I'm guessing. OK, let's remove a finger and see if that clears your head." The Manager pulled a pair of pliers from his back pocket and snipped them a couple of times in the air, demonstrating his familiarity and skill at using them.

"No!" He finally shouted. "Sorry no. I've not seen this person."

"You didn't sound certain before, perhaps we should take a finger, just in case."

"I mean I've seen him round here, but not for a couple of months at least."

The Manager thought for a moment then shrugged. The two thugs let go and he staggered backwards. "Thank you very much for your time. Of course if you *do* see him you'll let me know, *won't you?*" He threw a business card into the box of flowers, then tucked the pliers away. The Manager flashed a glance at the two heavies and left.

He sighed heavily and sat back against the wall, feeling a weight lifted from his shoulders. He hadn't had a cigarette for a couple of hours, but now seemed an appropriate moment. Reaching into his jacket pocket he found he didn't have one, or a jacket for that matter. Looking down he saw he was wearing a dark grey jumper, ripped at the shoulder. He reached quickly for his wallet in his trousers. There was no wallet and his trousers were made of worn-out, brown corduroy, way too big and falling apart. He staggered to his feet and ran to the nearest shop window to get a glimpse of what he was wearing. There was an off-license a couple of doors down and between the special offer posters he could just make out his own reflection. Sure enough, he was dressed roughly, as if he'd been living on the streets for years. But his attention quickly focused on his face; it was different, not his own. It wasn't hugely different, but it wasn't him.

He had indeed changed.

Dance with the Daffodils
Karen Ette

Paige stepped carefully down the narrow steps from the bookshop, pushing a leather-bound volume into the bag that was slung over her shoulder with one hand whilst holding her hat in place with the other. She walked briskly along the street avoiding the foul-smelling piles of rotting vegetables and animal waste, as she made her way home. The stench from the last shop nauseated her and once past the stinking tripe dresser's she looked all around to make sure there was no-one in sight then lifted her skirt and, still clutching her hat, ran along the Grasmere lanes. She stopped occasionally to check she hadn't been seen, as it would be unseemly for a young lady to be running. Whoever had owned the ankle boots before her must have had wider feet than she, as they were roomy and the leather soft, although the small heels snagged in the soft earth. The setting sun cast an orange glow across the water as she approached the lake, which was dark and still, reflecting the bare branches of the trees that surrounded it. Paige paused for a moment to catch her breath. She studied the lake; there were a few early daffodils close to the water's edge and a boat floating in the middle. Gentle waves lapped rhythmically along the shore. The sun sank lower and Paige continued up the slight rise to their cottage. She pushed open the gate, which creaked as if the movement was painful. When she was halfway up the path she had a feeling of being watched. Slowing her pace to something more sedate she continued and from the corner of her eye saw a figure hurrying along the other side of the hedge towards Dove Cottage. From the woman's profile she recognised her near neighbour, Dorothy. Paige smoothed her skirt before pushing open the cottage's heavy oak door. The smell of wood smoke met her as she stepped inside.

"I'm home," she called.

"In here," came Wesley's reply from the front parlour. She removed her hat and shrugged the heavy, woollen cape from her shoulders before joining him the warm room. Wesley was standing by the fire, holding a glass containing his favourite malt whisky. A balding gentleman, whose grey sideburns framed his kindly face, rose to his feet and dipped his head towards her.

"Good evening, Miss Paige," her neighbour greeted. She looked at Wesley who raised his eyebrows and gave a slight nod, so she dipped her knees in a curtsy, noticing that Wesley was struggling to hide his amusement at her awkwardness.

"Good evening, Mr Wordsworth," she answered, "I trust you are in good health." The older gentleman inclined his head and returned to his chair. Paige looked at Wesley, her eyes wide with enquiry.

"Mr Wordsworth has come to ask for my help, he was just about to explain when you arrived. Please carry on, sir." Wordsworth paused for a moment and looked towards Paige, who sat down on a high-backed chair by the window. She noticed Wesley's moustache twitch as he tried not to smile at the discomfort, which had now transferred from her to Wordsworth.

"It is my housekeeper that needs your help," he began, "or perhaps I should be clearer and say her niece. She is, quite wrongfully, in prison and if we cannot prove her innocence, she will hang."

"When did you come to know this?" Wesley asked.

"Yesterday, when our housekeeper told Dorothy."

"What is her crime?"

"She is accused of theft from her employer."

"And who would that be?"

"Mr Huxat."

"Up at the big house? Didn't his wife die recently?" Paige enquired. Wordsworth gave an almost unnoticeable jerk at her intervention and carried on directing his speech towards Wesley."

"Sarah stands accused of stealing a valuable necklace from Lady Huxat."

"But you can't hang for seating a necklace in this day and age." Paige was about to stand when Wesley inclined his head in a way that Paige knew she should remain seated. "I'm afraid, my sweet, that in *this* day and age one most certainly can hang for theft," he told her. "And where is the necklace?" Wesley asked Wordsworth.

"No-one seems to know."

"Can we be certain that Sarah did not steal the necklace?"

Wordsworth shrugged. "I fear not; I only have her aunt's word."

"Then we should ask her," Paige said, and a tingle of excitement ran through her veins as if someone were tickling her nerves with a feather.

"It isn't a place fit for a young lady," Wordsworth said, "but if you feel it would help," he turned to Wesley, "then please talk to the girl."

*

"Make haste, it's beginning to rain," Paige said holding on to her hat as an accompanying gust of wind threatened to pluck it away.

"You shouldn't have come," Wesley told her as they made their way towards the prison gates.

"Try and stop me." Paige was as animated as a spring lamb.

"Then you must conduct yourself in a ladylike manner. Remember, this is 1802."

"I know." Paige stood on tiptoe and kissed Wesley's rain-flecked cheek.

"Stop it!" Wesley scolded.

"No-one saw."

"Well, someone might have done, and it's improper behaviour," Wesley scolded and she felt his hand slide tenderly down her back. When they arrived, Wesley took a sheaf of papers from the inside pocket of his coat and banged on a dark door that was clad in ironwork. A panel slid back and a voice that sounded as though its owner had been gargling with grit snarled through the small opening:

"Well, what is your business?"

"We are here to question Miss Sarah Tickner."

"And who are you?"

"I am Miss Tickner's legal representative and I have with me a nurse who has to ensure she is being well cared for." Wesley waved the papers in front of the hatch, which slid shut. Bolts were drawn, a key turned and the door opened. They stepped inside and the door crashed to behind them, its bolts were slid back across and the key turned in the lock, and removed. Wesley raised his hat to the man with the gravelly voice who stood before them.

"Would you be so kind as to take me to Miss Tickner?"

Paige shivered as she took in her surroundings. The gaoler led them across a muddy yard and into a building so dark that she kept on bumping into Wesley as they made their way along a dank corridor. The place stank of sweat and human excrement. Paige covered her nose and mouth with her scarf keeping well away from the cells. One man spat at the gaoler as he passed, but missed so he shouted abuse instead. Sarah was in a cell at the end of the gloomy corridor. She was sitting on a bale of straw, her hair matted and her face puffy from crying.

"Ten minutes," the gaoler said, as he unlocked the cell, "no more." Wesley nodded and stepped inside. Paige followed him and the metal door closed behind them.

"Who are you?" Sarah asked, her eyes appearing wide with fright.

"You haven't come to take me already, surely. It isn't time yet." She began to shake and Paige watched her tears slide a trail down her dirty cheeks.

"It's all right, we are here to help you." Paige sat beside her on the straw bale.

"How can you help me? The Master says I stole Katherine's, I mean Mrs Huxat's, necklace and it's his word 'gainst mine. The Assizes have already decided I'm to hang." Her thin body trembled and Paige put her arm around Sarah's bony shoulders.

"Miss Tickner," Wesley said softly. "Did you take the necklace?"

"No! Well, yes, but I was given it; I didn't steal it."

"Who gave it to you?"

Paige felt Sarah beginning to shake more. She held her tighter and looked up at Wesley who had his notebook in one hand and his favourite *Montblanc* pen in the other. Paige tilted her head slightly, indicating the pen, but Wesley winked and grinned; she knew he would have it back in his pocket before the gaoler returned.

"Please tell us what happened, Sarah. We shall need to know everything if we are to help you," Paige said, but stopped when she heard a noise from the far corner of the cell. "What's that?" she whispered.

"It's a woman who just sits in the corner and snores," Sarah whispered back.

"Never mind her," Wesley moved to stand between them and the woman, "just tell us what happened."

"Mrs Huxat liked me and took me from being a chamber maid to look after her."

"Like a lady's maid?" Paige asked.

"Yes, she learnt me to read a bit, but then she started to get ill and I spent all my time feeding her, well trying to, and washing her, making her comfy. Then Mr Huxat would bring their bedtime drinks to her room before retiring. I'd go home once he was with her and come back the next morning." The young girl looked at Paige and her words caught in her throat as she continued. "She took ever so ill. Then she couldn't hang on any longer and she just faded away."

"But what about the necklace?" Wesley prompted, "When did she give it to you?"

"Three days afore she died. I'd washed her hair, although it had started to fall out, and dressed her as best I could and I went to put the necklace on her, but she stopped me. She put her hand on mine and said 'no, you must have this; it's my gift to you.' Well I said I couldn't do that, but she beckoned me close and whispered in my ear that it had been her mother's and it wasn't to be left where Mr Huxat could take it. I said that as he was a man, surely he had no need for it." Sarah paused and shook her head. "I could see she were getting weaker, but I never expected her to die. I thought she would get better, but I think she knew."

"Knew what?" Wesley bent towards Sarah.

"Knew that she were gonna die. Anyroad, she said she didn't want Mr Huxat's fancy woman getting her mother's necklace, so she wanted me to have it. She pressed it into my hands and smiled at me. I kissed her on her forehead and took the necklace."

"Do you know what she died from? Had she been ill for long?" Paige asked.

"No, she went downhill very quickly. It were pitiful to see her like that."

"Like what?" Paige took her arm away and held Sarah's dirty hands in hers.

"Please, Miss Tickner," Wesley said, "we really need to know."

Sarah nodded and casting her eyes down, carried on.

"She started 'avin' headaches and were always tired. Then her tummy got angry."

"Angry?" Paige asked. Sarah shuffled on the straw.

"Aye, angry. She had, you know…"

"Diarrhoea?" Wesley asked. Sarah nodded.

"Then she were as sick as a dog. She just kept on and on and it were full of blood. She were in such pain, holdin' on to her stomach and crying."

"Was there anything else, anything at all?" Wesley said, straightening up.

"Her finger nails went funny," Sarah said, looking at her own, dirty fingers.

"Funny, how?" Paige prompted.

"They had like white lines all over them."

"What did you do with the necklace?" Wesley asked.

"I pawned it in Keswick. It were no use to me. Then after Mrs

Huxat's funeral, I were arrested."

"Time's up!" The gaoler had come back and was unlocking the cell door.

"Thank you," Paige said and stood up. "Please take my coat, you are frozen."

"No, Miss, I can't." Sarah got to her feet. "They'll 'ave it off me, see, so there's no point."

Paige looked from the woman in the dark corner to the gaoler, who was pointing to the open door. She took off her scarf and gently wrapped it around Sarah's neck. "Very well, but we shall prove your innocence," she promised and followed Wesley out of the cell.

*

Paige saw the familiar figure of Dorothy walking along the lane as she made her way home from the village. She quickened her pace, but didn't run, and caught up with her neighbour. The lake was calm and empty as they passed by it.

"I wonder where the boat has gone," Paige said, shielding her eyes from the sunlight.

"I expect Mr Huxat's gamekeeper has tied it up proper to stop it drifting out onto the water," Dorothy said.

"Look at the lovely daffodils." Paige pointed to a cluster of yellow beside the lake.

"'Tis a lovely time of year, especially here in Westmoreland." Dorothy, too, shielded her eyes. "When William and I were at Glencoyne Bay, near Ulleswater, we saw a long belt of them along the shore. I never saw daffodils so beautiful, they were ever dancing, ever changing, in the breeze. I wrote about them in my diary. I'd like William to write one of his poems about them, but he doesn't seem too desirous at the moment."

"I'm sure he will." Paige smiled at Dorothy and then asked: "Do you know anything of gardening, Dorothy?"

"I do love my garden. What is it you are enquiring of?"

"Well, when I was in the alchemist's shop, getting Wesley's moustache wax, Mr Huxat's gardener came in and said he wanted some of that stuff to kill the dandelions. I thought it peculiar that he would buy weed killer from an alchemist."

"Not really, you can buy all sorts from there. That's where William's friend, Samuel, gets his opium for his aching back."

"Goodness me," Paige was surprised, but tried not to show how much.

"I have a rather nice printed work about gardens, which you would be most welcome to borrow if you would like to."

"Oh, yes please, that is most kind," Paige said and followed Dorothy into Dove Cottage.

*

Paige didn't move when Wesley came into the front parlour.

"What are you studying?" he asked.

Paige looked up from the table where a lamp stood casting light over two open books. She got up and before Wesley could remove his scarf, flung her arms around his neck and pressed her warm lips against his cold ones.

"I think I shall venture into Keswick more often," Wesley breathed as they moved apart.

"Did you find the necklace?" Paige asked.

"I found the pawnbroker, but he sold it on as Miss Tickner was never going to be able to pay back the money."

"Do you know who bought it?"

"He wouldn't say." Wesley stroked his moustache.

"Oh, I have your wax," Paige told him, "and I think Mrs Huxat was poisoned."

"Poisoned? With what?" Wesley poured himself a glass of malt whisky.

"Arsenic!"

"Arsenic?"

"Yes. I think Mr Huxat's gardener was buying it to use as a weed killer and when Mr Huxat took the bedtime drinks to his wife's room, hers was laced with arsenic. All of her symptoms fit, even the white lines on her fingernails. Everything is in this book of common ailments that I bought by mistake the other day. She picked up the leather-bound volume. "I thought it was by John Buchan; I really enjoyed *The Thirty-Nine Steps* and wanted to read more of his writing."

Wesley took the book and laughed; a loud, belly-laugh that invited Paige to join in. "Oh my sweetness." Wesley recovered himself, "he won't have been born yet. *The Thirty Nine Steps* was about the Great War in 1915. This is by Dry William Buchan." Paige took the book from him.

"Then it's a good thing that I made the mistake as arsenic poisoning is in here and that, along with a piece in Dorothy's garden manual that tells you how to kill weeds with it, confirms that she was indeed poisoned."

"And how are we going to prove it?" Wesley asked.

"Oh, you'll think of something," Paige said and slipped her arms around Wesley's waist, drawing him close once more.

*

Paige tugged at the neck of her dress.

"Sarah is much smaller than me," she said as she tried to find more room in her attire.

"You know where to go when we get there, don't you?" Wesley asked.

"Indeed I do," Paige answered and caught Wesley's hand in hers. The long tree-lined pathway that led to the Manor House was edged with purple violets and yellow celandines. "Listen to the birds chattering," she said, still pulling on her neckline. Their boots scrunched on the stones as they approached the house. Wesley had let Paige's hand go and was making his way towards the front door. Paige turned to her left and followed a well-worn path that led to the kitchens. She slipped through the open scullery door and crept quietly along a dim passageway.

"Who are you?" The lady who stood before Paige wore black and had a set of keys on a chatelaine attached to her belt.

"I'm Sarah Tickner's replacement," Paige answered and bent her knees in a curtsy.

"The Master never mentioned any replacement," the woman, who Paige assumed was the Housekeeper, challenged.

"Oh. I was told to come here and do housemaids' duties."

"Very well, you can begin by cleaning the grates. Do the Master's study first, that's opposite the Library just off the entrance hall, and then work your way around the downstairs rooms before going upstairs You'll find all you need in there." She pointed to a large broom cupboard behind Paige. "Don't go into the Mistress's room. No-one is allowed in there."

'I won't need to go anywhere near the Mistress's room,' Paige thought, 'you have given me the exact place I need to be.'

"Yes, Ma'am, I mean no, Ma'am," Paige answered, gave another curtsy and turned around. She heard the Housekeeper's footsteps receding and, after a swift glance over the cupboard's contents, snatched up a bucket, brush, some black-lead and a few old rags, then made her way to Mr Huxat's study. She could hear the rumbling of deep voices coming from the Library and smiled, knowing that Wesley was keeping Mr Huxat's attention away from the room opposite.

Putting the cleaning paraphernalia down, she began her exploration of the study, pushing the items she was seeking into the pocket of her apron as she completed her search. She noticed the voices becoming louder and less muffled. Lifting the bucket, she made her way back to the scullery and out into the spring sunshine once more. Walking briskly away from the house and into the lane, she waited for Wesley to join her. After only a few minutes she heard his boots thudding on the ground and stepped out from the shelter of the hedgerow. He swept her up in his arms and she kissed him as if he had been away on a crusade.

"Did you get it?" Wesley asked and put her down. She tapped her pocket and nodded.

"What time did you tell him?" she asked.

"Mid-day." Wesley took out his pocket watch. "That gives us three hours," he said then replaced the watch and twisted his moustache.

"You're enjoying this, aren't you?" Paige said and took his hand as they made their way back to their cottage.

*

Wesley was standing behind Paige so that he could shield her from the cool breeze that had picked up. She felt distinctly chilly as they stood beside the lake and beneath the trees. A movement further round the lake's edge heightened her senses and she knew from the change in his stance that Wesley had seen it too. They waited in their concealed spot until they heard voices, raised voices. Two men were standing next to the moored rowing boat, arguing.

"Right on time," Wesley said, "come on," and he stepped into view. "Is this what you are looking for?" he shouted over to the men who turned towards them.

"You!" Richard Huxat almost spat at Wesley, who was holding a sapphire necklace in his right hand.

"It was a careless thing to leave it in a rowing boat, albeit concealed." Wesley told him.

Paige noticed Huxat's colour rising until his face appeared almost purple.

"It's mine!" the man with Huxat shouted. "You promised it to me! You told me to be here at mid-day to collect it."

"I did not. He gave me your message to meet here at mid-day."

Richard Huxat pointed to Wesley. The two men looked at each other and then back to Wesley.

"Huxat, you owe me. That necklace is mine." The other man growled.

"And why might that be, Dry Musgrove?" Wesley enquired.

"For signing his wife's death certificate. He said that if I confirmed she died from natural causes he would give me her necklace."

"But she gave it to Sarah Tickner, didn't she, Huxat?"

"And I bought it back," Huxat sneered, "so you've nothing on me. Hand it over."

"There is just the small matter of murder." Wesley moved the necklace from Richard Huxat's reach.

"That's preposterous," Huxat snapped.

Paige produced a small, brown bottle from her pocket and said: "I think this may prove otherwise." She smiled and handed the bottle to Wesley.

"Where did you get that?" Huxat spat the words at Paige.

"It was in your study when I cleaned it this morning."

"I think the constables should have this, don't you, Huxat?" Wesley said and beckoned to the law enforcement officers who had been standing close by and behind Huxat and the Doctor, hidden by a large evergreen shrub.

*

"Thank you for everything you have done," William Wordsworth lifted his teacup as if giving a toast. "Miss Tickner and her family are extremely grateful."

"It was our pleasure." Paige raised her cup in response. "Oh, I almost forgot, here is your book, Dorothy. It was most helpful, thank you." She turned to William. "You must write that poem Dorothy told us about."

"Which poem?" Wordsworth looked bemused.

"The one about the daffodils. Dorothy wrote about them in her diary when you went to Ulleswater."

"Yes, I think I shall." William nodded.

"Thank you for the tea," Wesley said, "I think it's time we left."

Paige walked with Wesley along Dove Cottage's path and through the garden gate, closing it behind them. They both stopped and turned; William was running after them.

"Wait, you've forgotten your gloves," he was calling. He arrived at the gate and looked directly at them. Paige wanted to reach out to him, but knew he couldn't see her, or Wesley; all he would see was a pair of ladies' boots, a jar of moustache wax and a copy of *The Thirty-Nine Steps*, lying on the grass next to a clump of golden daffodils. [1]

---

[1] *The Thirty-Nine Steps* by John Buchan first appeared as a serial in *Blackwood's Magazine* in August and September 1915 before being published in book form in October that year.

A Gift in Spring
Donna Shepherd

The trees outside the Tranquil Times care home had lost their naked appearance and had started to bud. The ground underneath was covered in a blanket of green and within days the first crocuses would appear. Fay blinked and stared. "When had that happened?" she mused. Soon it would be Easter. Fay loved springtime: the promise of new life and a feeling that the world was waking up after a long sleep.

She turned the car engine off, sat back in her seat for a moment and gazed out of the window. Her job in the care home kept her busy and she had always enjoyed the time after Christmas – residents had seen their families, usually more than they had all year, and the members of staff were more relaxed after some time with theirs.

For Fay however, Christmas meant double shifts. She always volunteered so that her colleagues could enjoy some time off, and besides, the extra cash was more than welcome. She was tired but the thought of spending the following day on the sofa with Bert, her greyhound, soothed her.

"Come on, only one more day to go," Fay said to herself. Taking a deep breath she left the sanctuary of her car and walked into the building.

Fay looked at the pictures on the wall in front of her. The smiling face of Mrs Read was instantly recognisable amongst the solemn and forlorn expressions worn by the other residents. Mrs Read was Fay's favourite, mainly because despite being in pain she never complained and always had a smile on her face.

Picking up her list of duties for the day Fay made her way out of the office and turned left along the corridor. She stopped outside number two and tapped quietly on the door.

"Good morning, Mrs Read," she said as she pushed the door open and stepped into the room.

"Good morning, Fay dear," replied Mrs Read from her chair by the window. "I'm so glad you're here," she said looking up from her paper. "Sally was in earlier and refused to open the window for me. Will you do it, dear? I feel so pedestrian in my life and hate not being able to do things for myself anymore." She sighed. "I can see the garden," Mrs Read continued, "but I can't smell it and I do so love this time of year." Pausing, she picked up the vase of daffodils that were on the table beside her. "These are so beautiful," she said, "such a wonderfully happy colour and something I really thought I wouldn't see again. Thank you so very much for bringing them."

"You're very welcome and don't be daft," said Fay, "It's going to take a lot more than a heart-attack to finish you off."

Mrs Read smiled. "Right you are my dear. There is no point being worried and best to just get on. You are a wonderful girl. I really do not know what I'd do without your company," she exclaimed, before asking, "how is Bert doing?"

Fay laughed as she unlatched the window and pushed it open. "He's fine and no doubt curled up in the middle of my bed as I speak. What are you watching today?"

"Oh some rubbish about how to wear denim," Mrs Read replied. "I thought there would be a limit as to the amount of this daytime drivel that I could tolerate but every day I turn it on and off I go again." Fay smiled as she quickly and expertly changed the bed. "It's aimed at people who are more than content to simply sit and stare at the television. What we need is to get you a good box set." Box sets had become a passion for Fay, the way the stories continued, twisting and turning as the plots grew ever more complicated. "I can bring you something to watch if you'd like, maybe the first series of Dexter would stop you being bored."

Mrs Read laughed, a lovely tinkling sound. "That sounds right up my street, murder for revenge and justified bloodshed. Will I be able to play it on my television?"

Fay stopped what she was doing and walked over to the television. "Yes, you have a dvd player in the television set so we can just slide the discs in and press play. There are ten hours on the first disc so I'll bring it in tomorrow."

Mrs Read grinned. "Well you'd better, I simply don't know how many hours I've got left," she said in her matter of fact way. "How many discs are there?"

Fay looked up at her from her position on her knees "Ten," she replied. "No point worrying about that – you just get to sit still and watch them all." Mrs Read sighed, "It sounds like a fantastic way of spending what time I have left. Maybe it'll give me a few ideas regarding that scheming daughter-in-law of mine." Fay met Mrs Read's gaze and both women chuckled.

*

"It's just so bloody inconvenient," Annette was saying to Matron, in her high pitched nasal tone, as Fay walked into the office. "What with David working abroad the role of carer falls directly onto me and while I'd never complain," she said, sighing deeply, "she is family after all, but the expectation and pressure it puts me under is simply too much."

Annette walked over to the window, her back to the room. "Of course," she said, "if I had some kind of time frame to work with – well then, that would make life so much easier."

Fay stifled a gasp while Matron leant forward on her desk.

"Am I correct in understanding that you would like me to hazard a guess as to how much longer your mother-in-law has to live?" Matron said her tone dangerously low.

Annette swung around, oblivious to Matron's attitude and with relief plainly visible on her face. "Oh I knew you'd understand," she said. "It's never-ending this waiting lark, and the term fees are astronomical. I've tried to talk to David but he was never wholly in favour of that school...." Annette stopped talking and after a quick glance at the ceiling continued. "I'm sure you can appreciate the pressure on me Matron, as a mother yourself," she said with a pointed glance at Fay. "The money that David sends has to cover all manner of expenses and Benja's school fees are additional."

"I take it that David is still unaware of the school situation?" Matron asked.

Annette looked at the floor before meeting Matron's gaze. "I just want what is best for my boy and that school, despite the cost, is what is best. David will come round when he sees the results for himself."

Fay hid a grin. It was no secret that Benja had already started at the much coveted private boys" school, and that David knew nothing of this arrangement having previously forbidden his enrolment.

Fay remembered that David had flown home after his mother's heart-attack and Annette had deemed that a good time to discuss their son's education. Her timing could not have been worse and their raised voices could be heard throughout the care home. She and Sally had huddled together in the corridor as David and Annette had argued over the bed in which Mrs Read lay.

"But I don't want our son to attend just any school," Annette had argued. "He deserves to mingle with the best, not the common riffraff and the curriculum is…"

David had cut her off in mid-sentence. "I do not want to hear it," he had shouted. "Our son will be better equipped to deal with the harsh reality of life after mixing with the so called riffraff you appear to fear so much. Jesus Christ, woman, you'd think we had money pouring out of the bath taps the way you talk."

David had stormed out of his mother's room but Annette had grabbed his arm, leaving the door half open. "Surely that's all going to change very soon" she said, "the Doctor very much doubts your mother will survive this," Annette continued, "and she would want her money to benefit dear Benja."

Fay had heard every word and remembered David, silent, pale and trembling, as he had left his mother's room and walked past her.

*

Back in the office, Annette sighed and turned to look out of the window. "Life is so hard with David away," she said, "and all I want for Benja is a happy future. Surely that is not too much to ask?"

Matron coughed and glanced at Fay. "Mrs Read has been confined to the limitations of her room for a while now, but it is only her physical self that is deteriorating. Her mind is still very much alert and she is perfectly able to engage in prolonged and deeply-thought out discussions."

Annette sniffed. "Yes," she said, "I'm perfectly aware of her mental state. Indeed," she continued, eyebrows raised dramatically, "Dr. Hawkins lost no time in telling me that she must have an extraordinarily strong determination to live." Annette turned her attention to the floor as she muttered, "further evidence that the old bat is simply staying alive to irritate me personally."

"Anyway, the point is I get that her mind works, but surely her body can't go on much longer?" Annette said. "Could you maybe hazard a guess?"

"I really couldn't say," Matron said through clenched teeth. "Now if you'll excuse me I have my rounds to complete." Matron stood up and strode to the door, wrenching it open so forcibly that it banged against the wall. Annette turned back to face the two women. Her face had resumed its stony expression and, head high, she stalked out of the room.

As the door slammed shut behind her Fay let out a deep breath. "Bloody hell, the cheek of that woman!" she exclaimed.

"I know," Matron sighed. "Of all the daughters-in-law in the world and Mrs Read got her! Still," she continued, "at least Mrs Read is well enough to see Mr Johnson today. I'll call him now that Annette has left and tell him the coast is clear. He said that he had written the day out in his diary for her so he won't mind the time," she grinned at Fay. "That's the benefit of having a family lawyer I suppose," she said, moving over to her desk and picking up the phone, "and Mrs Read will be so pleased that she can get her affairs properly in order without interference."

"Do you think we should contact David?" Fay asked.

"I believe that he knows and fully supports whatever it is his mother intends to do with her will," Matron answered. "It's not for the likes of us to question. Right, off you go while I make this call," she said, dismissing Fay from the room.

*

Fay placed both hands on the mattress and looked around the empty room. Without warning she sank onto her knees and began to sob, hard and unrestrained, the sound echoing in the silence.

The door clicked softly shut behind her.

"Fay, can I come in?" David asked.

Sniffing, Fay stood up and turned away from the bed.

"Yes of course," she replied, wiping her nose with a tissue from her pocket. "It's your, I mean was your, mother's room." She paused and met his gaze. "I'm so very sorry; your mother was such a wonderful person and I shall miss her," she said.

"Thank you," David replied. "I know you meant the world to her and kept her smiling despite her suffering. If there is anything I can do for you, please do not hesitate to ask. Ok?"

Fay moved over to the window and smiled. "Your mother loved the garden here," she said, then asked, "have you thought about putting a bench out there as a memorial to her?"

"What a great idea," David said. "That simply would not have occurred to me and mother would love it!" He took a deep breath and joined Fay by the window. "There is something else," he said. "Mother wanted you present at the reading of her will. It's at two o'clock tomorrow and will be held in Matron's office."

"Why on earth would she have wanted me there?" Fay asked with a worried expression on her face.

"I really couldn't say, but I certainly wouldn't worry about it," David said, patting her awkwardly on the arm. "Now if you'll excuse me I must be going. There is so much to sort out."

David paused at the door and turned to Fay. "Did you know that my wife had enrolled Benja at Landsborough Boys?" he asked.

Fay looked at her hands, aware of the fact that she was blushing.

"Yes, I did," she answered, "and I'm sorry I didn't tell you. Matron thought it none of our business."

David nodded and left the room.

*

"To my Grandson, Benja Read, I leave thirty thousand pounds which is to be placed in trust until his thirtieth birthday, upon which date he can have complete control over the full amount including all interest accrued." Mr Johnson read from the document that he held in his hand.

"Oh how wonderfully kind, how very thoughtful of her," Annette said, then turning to David, "but why can't he inherit that now?"

"I have no idea," he replied. "Please go on Mr Johnson," he said to the man sitting behind Matron's desk.

Taking a deep breath, Mr Johnson continued: "To the woman who has been my sole companion these last five years, a woman who has made my final years so bearable, I leave…."

Annette fidgeted in her seat and leaned forward. "Yes, Mr Johnson," she interrupted, "it is true that I have been a most constant friend to my dear mother-in-law."

Mr Johnson stared at Annette then looked at the document in his hand. "I leave" he continued, "fifty thousand pounds to Fay Bennett."

Annette screamed and flopped back in her chair, her mouth opening and closing in rapid succession.

"What?" she yelled. "There has to be some mistake. It is I who has been here day after day, week after week, tending to her needs, being a friend to her…"

"Shut up, Annette," David said to his wife. "We all know that not one word of that is true. Is there anything else, Mr Johnson?" he asked the solicitor who was surveying the room with a bemused look on his face.

"Erm, yes," he replied. "The local greyhound rescue centre is to receive twenty thousand pounds." Mr Johnson coughed. "You all know how she felt about those poor creatures." He paused, and then said, "The house is yours David. Solely yours, to do with as you please."

Fay watched as David stood and turned to his wife who was staring at the solicitor as if he had grown two heads. "A care assistant and a dogs" home? A bloody dogs" home?" she screamed, "Are you all raving mad? What about my boy? What about his fees?" She gulped and glanced up at her husband. "I was going to tell you, straight after his first report. You'll see how fantastic…"

"For God's sake shut up, woman," David said, "I will not hear another word about it. You can stay in the house until we sell it, but I suggest that you start looking at the local comprehensives. Your maintenance won't stretch to private school fees. Mother told me her plans months ago, right after her heart-attack– not a penny of her money was to benefit you – those were her wishes and those wishes will stand." David turned to leave the room but stopped at the door.

"Oh and by the way, I want a divorce. My solicitor will be in touch."

David nodded at Matron as he passed her, but stopped in front of Fay.

"I hope that you will be very happy," he said, "Mother held you in the highest regard and if this money in any way helps you then I will be a happy man. Goodbye, dear Fay."

Betrayal
Melinda Ingram

"So where did you get to this morning, then?" asked Ali, as she and Mike approached the centre of Great Glen, the village they lived in.

It was just before six in the evening and people were shopping on their way home, perhaps from work, or from a day out. They pulled up behind a red Astra that was reversing out of the Post Office car park onto Main Street, before manoeuvring round a couple of pedestrians to take its place on the forecourt. Mike flipped the door handle as he answered, and part of what he'd said was lost to Ali as they emerged on different sides of the car; "...then I just popped in here to get my passport renewal checked," she heard. "It'll be good to get away."

Ali, too, was looking forward to their holiday in Spain that June. She followed her husband across the car park, catching his hand. His eyes crinkled at the sides.

"Two cards, and two pressies, right?"

There were buckets of cut daffodils outside on the steps up to the doors, some large and yellow, some with small orange trumpets, and others almost white with feathered centres. There were tulips in multi-coloured bunches of red, yellow and lilac, spring flowers ready for Mothering Sunday, the next day. The windows were enticing, showing heart shaped biscuits hanging on ribbons, boxes of chocolates and many other things.

They spent some time laughing at silly verses in cards and even sillier pictures, and eventually chose one for each of their Mums, a flowery one for his and a funny one about taking some time out for hers. Quickly assessing what else was available, such as jewellery, stationary and delicatessen goodies, Ali chose two scarves from a tastefully arranged display.

"I'll pay for these," she told Mike, taking them to the counter, as she watched him diverting over to the sporting magazines.

"Evening, Ali. Had a good day?" The assistant stretched out her hand to take Ali's purchases, her eyes following Mike. "Hi, Gail," Ali greeted her friend, acknowledging her gaze. "He's about had enough," she said, grinning. "We've spent the whole afternoon looking at kitchen displays in town."

Gail deftly wrapped the scarves in tissue paper, having taken off the price tags, and slipped them into a thick swirly patterned paper bag with the cards. She took Ali's debit card from her and completed the transaction. "Got to keep 'em busy," Ali quipped. "See you in the morning, running shoes at the ready!"

"Yeah, see you," Gail called, and Mike pursed his lips in a kissing motion towards her as he followed Ali from the shop.

"Flirt!" Ali scolded, swiping Mike's arm as he grinned at her.

Getting back in the car a thought occurred to Ali. Some months back, October wasn't it, she had to get her passport redone in time for a few days away post-Christmas. She'd had to go up to Oadby because the Glen post office didn't offer the check and send service. Mike had lied. She looked sideways at his face and he smiled but didn't turn as they drove round the corner. "Yes?" he asked.

"Nothing, just thinking."

"Dangerous behaviour, thinking! You happy with the pressies, then?"

"Fine," Ali replied and lapsed into silence. He'd lied, surely? Why would he lie? A cold tight ball lay heavy in her stomach. She controlled her breathing to try to avoid panicking and blurting out something damaging. They had a pact. They always told each other the truth. It was part of their solid foundation. They were supposed to always tell each other their worries, too, but somehow Ali just couldn't ask.

They pulled up on the driveway, and Ali looked back at the car as Mike opened the red front door. Then she was straight into the kitchen to make a quick supper before an evening of ironing in front of the box. Even though Mike suggested playing Scrabble together, or snuggling up and watching a film in bed Ali wouldn't let herself be drawn out.

*

The alarm beeped at 6.30, but Ali was already awake. She'd slept only fitfully as she'd imagined various scenarios for her husband's perfidy. That's what it was. Deceit! The smallest of details had revealed a deceit, which might not be so small. Mike could have been away for even a couple of hours. When he said he'd just been to Glen she knew that couldn't be true, and yet he had sent off the application because she'd seen some papers about it on the desk in his office, their smallest upstairs room. She pulled on her track suit, resisted leaning over for a kiss.

"Going now, back soon," she whispered at Mike's back and she retreated from the bedroom and ran down the stairs. Trusty running shoes on, bottle of water pushed into the holder on the back of her belt, pedometer strapped to her arm, she was out of the house and on the way to the park less than ten minutes after getting up.

Pictures of Mike up to no good replayed in her mind on the run, as they had been all night. She tried to dismiss them and concentrate on breathing in the fresh cold air and enjoying the watery sun that hadn't yet done much for the frost covered pavements.

"Hey, Ali! Looking good." Debs and Gail were jogging up and down, waiting for her and Val.

"Here's Val. Let's go down the bridle path and out round to Burton Overy." Ali had spotted the fourth member of their Sunday morning running club approaching from the opposite side of the park, skirting the brook.

For the first couple of miles they built a steady pace with little talk. Blackbirds sang in the pink blossomed trees and dog walkers offered the occasional "morning". This was a regular route. Reaching the wide corner of grass at the end of a road, which sported a bench designed for bus passengers, Debs and Val slowed down and sank onto the seat. Debs bent forward, head between her knees and Val leaned back watching Ali and Gail as they stretched their limbs, rubbing calves and breathing deeply.

"Half way round then. No hanging about today, though. I've got to get back and pamper myself ready for lunch out with the family. It's going to be great getting together."

"Nice one, Debs, What are you up to Ali?"

"Taking the Mums out," she replied. "But I'm not in the mood. I'm hoping this run's going to freshen me up and stop me stressing."

"What's up then?' asked Val, sitting up and putting her hand out to touch Ali's arm.

"Oh, I'm just being silly, probably. I think I caught Mike telling a lie."

"You worry, about nothing," Debs said, with a grin. "Men are always up to something. You just have to let them get on with it. Means nothing and allows them a bit of drama."

"Mike and I have always been straight with each other, but I can't seem to ask him. He was out yesterday morning when I got back from the gym. He nearly always has a lie in, or potters around the house. Then I was in the shower when he got back, and then we went off to look at kitchens as planned, so it wasn't until later that I remembered and asked."

"Well, what did he say, then?"

"Yeah, what's the big lie? Out with it?"

Both Val and Debs encouraged her to spill the details.

"He said he'd gone to the Post Office to get his passport renewal checked."

"What's wrong with that?" Gail chipped in.

"He can't have, though, can he? I had to go up to Oadby only a while ago to do mine. You've never done Check-and-Send at Glen."

"But they do now, don't you Gail?" said Val, laughing.

"Yeah, since January. New Year, new jobs," Gail confirmed.

"You see," reassured Debs. "Worrying about nothing. You want something to really worry about. Then you'd know it, you idiot."

"God, I'm stupid," Ali sighed, a bubble of relief rising through her. "I've hardly slept all night, I've been so worried, but I might have known. Mike's a gorgeous guy. Come on let's get done."

She bent forward to retie the lace on her trainer as Val, Debs and Gail moved off down the grassy track running parallel to the pavement. Straightening up to follow her friends Ali's happy thoughts jarred as she caught Gail's words, directed at the other two.

"Yep, Mike's quite something," Gail mouthed, with the hint of a triumphant smile on her lips.

Far From Here
Stephen Ashurst

The sun was still quite low in the clear sky and a crisp, cold breeze chilled the morning air. Flowers were beginning to bloom in the borders around the edges of the small, gated city park. Gentle birdsong could be heard in the trees nearby, despite the sounds of impatient traffic in the distance. This would be a calming and tranquil place to spend time, but Brad hated it. He sat in the middle of the park bench, his heavy black woollen coat wrapped tightly around him. He slurped loudly on his morning coffee-in-a-cardboard-cup, but some of it went down the wrong way and he ended up coughing it up loudly and dribbling some of it onto the neat block-paved pathway. Right in front of him a small elderly lady with white, candy-floss hair and a brown tartan coat passed by, she was dragging a bright red trolley bag behind her, but stopped briefly for some frowning and judgmental tutting, before setting off again with an irritatingly shrill noise as the wheels turned.

"There you are!" Harriet's voice made him jump. "I thought we were meeting at the gate?" She looked far too bright and cheerful for this time of day. Even her yellow coat seemed to shout 'Get up and enjoy this beautiful fresh spring morning'. She jumped onto the park bench and sat on the backrest behind him, then leant down and kissed him on top of his head.

"Why did you want to meet here again? I hate this place," Brad replied.

"You hate everything, my grumpy goat. That's why I love you." He shrugged and continued eating. "Don't you want to know why I called you this morning?" She looked almost bouncy with excitement.

"You're going to tell me anyway I suppose."

"Well not if you're going to be like that."

Brad rolled his eyes and sighed. "Sorry, I don't like being up at this time if I can help it. Especially when it's cold like this. What did you want to tell me?"

"I read something on 'The Cult of 16' last night, they said that if you..."

"Why do you even read that shit? That website is run by freaks and weirdos with nothing better to do than invent stupid conspiracy theories. When was the last time anything they said turned out to be true?"

"Angel Heights housing block," she replied confidently.

"Angel Heights?" Brad drained his coffee cup and threw it in the direction of the old woman. "Everyone knew about Angel Heights. They might as well have stuck a sign on the door saying prostitutes, drugs and corrupt politicians inside."

"But how did everyone know about it? Rumours spread once people had seen it online." He dropped his head in his hands and gave a big sigh. "Whatever. There's a new thing they're calling 'Pandora', because once this stuff is out there there's no putting it back."

"Sounds like their usual crap, but go on."

"OK get this, the theory is that we are not really here, that this is an artificially generated world that we're all trapped inside."

"Oh my freakin'... this is their worst one yet. So you take the red pill then what happens? Eh?"

"I don't follow."

"This goes way beyond conspiracy theory, this is sci-fi, this is bad sci-fi! With the emphasis on fiction."

"That's what I thought until I read the test. It says that if you go to certain GPS co-ordinates and enter the right code on your phone then you will find the truth."

"Yeah, so where are the co-ordinates? Somewhere in remote Alaska no doubt."

"In this park; I checked online."

Brad opened his mouth then closed it again; that was not what he expected to hear. "Where in this park? That doesn't mean I believe any of this, I'm just curious."

"Well mister curious, it's just over there." She pointed in the direction the old woman had gone. "Not sure where exactly, but I've got the co-ordinates up on the map on my phone. So we can go and check it out." She pulled out her bright-pink smartphone and clicked the screen; it was already zoomed in on this part of town, with crosshairs where they were standing and a red marker at the far end of the park.

"Fine, let's do this so I can get back to some hard earned sleep."

Harriet skipped off eagerly, looking back with a sparkle in her eye, but Brad felt heavy getting up never mind moving and it wasn't long before she was out of sight. The main path twisted to the right into the heavy foliage of the old park trees. It was practically a tunnel, the lowest growth was trimmed and well kept, but the higher branches were left to grow together. The pathway twisted to the left before coming out into a circular clearing around a lichen-covered stone pond with a fountain in the middle. But there was no sign of Harriet.

"Harry!" he called out. No answer, so he ran round to the pathway disappearing into the tunnel of branches on the opposite side. Coming out at the other end he was at the far end of the park. The familiar tall and well-worn red brick wall ran across in front of him, to the right a path led past a small red and white workman's tent and into town, to the left was a path leading under a disused rail bridge to the back of the industrial estate on the edge of town. But there was still no sign of her. "Harry! Where are you?" He was about to head under the bridge when he heard a rustling noise.

"Shh." Harriet's head poked out of the tent, she beckoned anxiously to him.

"What are you doing in there?"

"It must be here; this is exactly where the co-ordinates lead." She whispered loudly before disappearing inside again. He stepped into the snug accommodation and immediately tripped over a toolbox in the doorway. He fell awkwardly onto a small chair, which tipped sideways and sent him head first into the corner of the tent. Harriet laughed as he tried to wriggle out sideways, but he'd got one arm through the chair and it was pinning him down. "Stylish entry." She said with a grin but didn't offer to help.

Brad rolled over and pulled himself sideways, managing to get himself off the upturned chair and onto the floor, narrowly missing Harriet's face with his foot. Finally, he managed to pull himself up to his feet and straighten the chair. He looked back and saw what he'd tripped over – a red trolley bag like the one the old woman had been pulling.

A couple of his fingers had been bent back, as had the nail on his thumb. It really hurt. He shook his hand in pain then held it out to Harriet. "Look at that will you, I broke a nail."

"You're such a woman."

"I am not!"

"Sit down and shut up." She waved a hand at the newly straightened chair opposite hers. He stuck his tongue out at her playfully but still felt his face glowing with embarrassment. He sat down very carefully to ensure no more mishaps. "OK so this is the location exactly, look at this." She held out her phone, zoomed in on this end of the park and sure enough they were right on top of the pin. I'm going to send a text to this number." She pulled a small yellow piece of paper from her pocket and held it out for Brad. "Would you mind?"

Brad took it and glanced over the number sequence. "1, 6, 2, 8, 3, 0, 0, 0, 0, 0, 0, 0, 2, 5, 3, 9, 3," he read aloud.

"OK, let me see so I know I've got it." He held it out while she checked each number meticulously. "Yep that's it. OK here goes." She clicked the send button and waited with a look of giddy excitement on her face. After a couple of seconds, the look dropped and she sighed.

"Come on, we've tried it and now we know it's just a load of…"

A beeping sound came from the far side of the small tent. Hovering just in front of the canvas on the far wall was a yellow glowing rectangle with three short horizontal lines inside. The internationally recognised hamburger icon, signifying a menu. They looked at each other for a moment, then Brad reached out to it.

"Wait!" Harriet shouted, slapping his hand away.

"What? You wanted to know the truth. Finally, we see something interesting and you don't want to see what it is."

"I do, I just want to be sure it's safe. No don't…" Brad reached out again and this time touched the menu button. There was a single beep and the yellow button expanded into a larger box where yellow glowing text appeared inside. The back of the tent was still visible behind this floating screen, but the light was bright enough to be easily readable against any background.

There was a cross icon in the top left of the screen and below were three buttons with text next to them.

[1] Environment settings
[2] Resident settings
[3] Exit

"What the hell?" Brad scratched his chin then touched the first option, a new set of options appeared with a scrollbar at the side. Feeling almost familiar with the interface now, Brad slid the scrollbar down to reveal hundreds of options. He clicked the one named 'Time'. The screen changed again, this time showing a circular dial with numbers, representing hours of the day. A solid triangle at the top pointed down between the numbers 9 and 10. Checking his watch it was indeed 9:30am.

"Stop it Brad, you're just clicking stuff and you've got no idea what it does."

"It won't do anything, this is someone's idea of a joke, look." He touched the top of the dial and slid it anti-clockwise; the numbers moved round the dial following the position of his finger. "See.

Look, if I move this round to put 0 at the top it should be midnight and dark." He slid the dial again, but just as he passed the number 18 the light outside did in-fact change and darken.

"What have you done? Put it back."

"No way, I want to see this." Brad stuck his head outside the little tent, which was only illuminated by the yellow glowing lines of the floating screen. "It's dark. Harry, look at this it is actually night time!" He stepped out into the clear and moonlit sky, the street lights towards town were flickering on. But as his eyes were adjusting to the light, the moon raced across the sky, only to be followed briefly by pink daylight coming up over the horizon. This lasted a split second before the sun stopped in the sky and bright daylight shone in his face again. The speed of this change had a dizzying effect and Brad stumbled backwards into the tent. "That was so trippy, I've never seen anything like it in my life! Harry you've got to try this, stand out there and I'll make the sun come up."

"Did you damage something when you hit your head?

"What are you on about?"

"I thought we were trying to be subtle here, and sneak into this little tent to see what's going on. Not shout it from the rooftops. People will have seen that! I don't know how anyone could have missed it to be honest. But anyone who actually knows what this thing is will definitely know we've been playing with it."

"I didn't think it was really going to do anything."

"Well it did. So what do we do? There could be people heading this way right now."

"OK." Brad rubbed the side of his head where he'd hit it on the chair, but realised he was using his painful hand. "Ow! OK I think we've got two options. We either make a run for it now, and don't stop till we're back at my place, or we click exit and see where this goes." He leant over and touched the little back arrow to bring the screen back to the original three options, then pointed at the 'exit' button.

"I don't like this. I know it was my idea to come here, but I wish you hadn't..." Brad put his hand up to silence her. There was a noise outside, a faint screeching sound followed by footsteps. Harriet stood up and reached out to grab hold of Brad, but then it went quiet. They both froze. Brad put a finger to his lips and held the other hand palm out to suggest she didn't move.

The door was whipped open and an angry shrivelled face intruded. Her light candy-floss hair seemed at odds with the sharp look in her eyes.

"What have you done?" She hissed through clenched teeth.

Harriet screamed and staggered backwards, grabbing Brad's shoulder for support. But Brad had turned away and found the screen still awaiting instruction. He quickly hit option three; 'exit'.

"No!" The voice hissed, but he couldn't see her, or even Harriet. Everything had gone black and all sound faded into the distance.

*

Brad gasped into consciousness, sitting up quickly and checking for signs of danger. He was in a clean but older looking hospital ward, perhaps 1950s in style. It was a narrow room with rows of empty beds along each side, about twenty in total. Bright sunlight streamed in through large windows, but there was a chill to the air. He pulled back the covers to reveal he was wearing a pale blue hospital gown, open at the back. There was a white towelling dressing gown on the chair next to him. He put this on quickly and rubbed his arms through it. Stepping onto the floor the cold almost stung his feet, luckily there were slippers under the chair, which he quickly put on. He shivered then stood up and walked towards the large window on the opposite wall. Outside there was an expanse of immaculate, short-cut green lawn, sloping gently down to a sizeable lake at the bottom, decorated with water lilies and elegant swans. Beyond this a grand ornate garden, colourful flower beds and well-kept box hedges were made into patterns that would not have been out of place at a grand stately home. Finally, there was a high red brick wall, bright and clean although well worn.

He could think of worse places to spend his time, if they fixed the heating, but what was this place and how did he get here?

"Good morning, would you like a cup of tea?" A friendly looking nurse, perhaps in her fifties, was holding a delicate white teacup and saucer. He didn't normally like tea, but for some reason this seemed appealing.

"Sure, why not." He smiled and took it from her, noticing the name Grace on the badge she wore on her immaculate white dress uniform. He took a sip and sighed, it tasted wonderful. Why didn't he drink this tea more often? "Thank you." He pondered over how to phrase his question but decided to just come out with it. "Where am I?"

"Don't worry, it can take a little while to adjust back to normal again. Just relax, everything will make sense soon." She smiled and turned to walk away, but stopped. "Oh, your companion is awake in the other ward. You can see her if you like." She nodded to a door at the end of the room.

"Thank you." He repeated. She must be referring to Harriet he thought. "I don't mean to be rude but why is she in a different room? There are plenty of beds here?"

"This is the male ward, she is in the female ward." The nurse turned on her heel and left.

He took another sip, then put his tea down before heading out. Beyond the door was a long corridor leading to the left. There were lots of white doors with round portal windows in them, but no signs. Opposite was another door leading to a room identical to the one he'd left. All beds were empty apart from the one in the middle. It was Harriet, she was sitting up in bed drinking a cup of tea.

"Harry!" He exclaimed as he burst through the door. "Where are we?"

"I've no idea, you pressed the button." She looked calm and at home in the bed, as if she'd been there for days. She was staring out of the window and sipping her tea.

"Wait, did you do something with your hair? It's blonde."

"No it isn't, I haven't been blonde since…" Harriet pulled a bit of hair in front of her eyes. "OK it is blonde."

"But you had dark hair this morning. Doesn't that freak you out?"

"Oh don't start that again, you always do this! You caused this mess, but you start judging me if I don't run around like a crazy person trying to sort it out." She practically threw her teacup down to turn and face him.

"I caused it? Excuse me but this was your idea in the first place. I would have been happily tucked up until the afternoon."

"Well you can't go back to your bed now, because you pressed the button. But I gather there are plenty of beds for you to sleep in here, so why don't you sod off and use one."

"Well maybe I will, or maybe I'll go and share one with nurse Grace. She looks like she knows a few…"

"Ahem" A staged cough came from behind him. Brad turned and saw the disapproving but somehow still friendly face of nurse Grace.

"I didn't mean you! Not that there's anything wrong with you, at all. But I wasn't really meaning… You know, I was joking and er. Yeah."

"Eloquently put, thank you," nurse Grace replied with a polite and patient smile. "The doctor will be coming to give you your revival medicine shortly. You have about fifteen minutes but then you need to be back in your own beds." Then she left the room.

"Nice going, Casanova," Harriet said teasing him. Brad turned just in time to catch a pillow with his face. He grinned and picked up a pillow from the nearest bed and started prowling towards her. "Don't you dare, I'm in hospital resting." She replied, also with a big grin.

"Then I'll have to give you a good dose of something else." He leapt over the beds between them and went for her with his pillow raised, but was stopped by a familiar screeching noise behind him. He frowned and lowered his pillow, only to be whacked again by another one from Harriet. "Stop it." He said, grabbing the pillows and throwing them behind the bed. He turned to see a little old lady pushing a tea trolley, with a wobbly wheel, which seemed to screech as she pushed it along. She had white, candy floss hair and a forced smile.

"Cup of tea, dears?" It was the old woman from the park, dressed as a tea lady.

"No we've already got drinks, but thank you." Harriet said hesitantly. Brad glanced back at her. She looked worried and obviously recognised her too.

"Are you... following us?" Brad asked.

"Shut up you idiot!" She hissed. "Don't speak like you know me." Then forced a smile back onto her aged face.

"But I only clicked the exit button. I didn't know what it would do."

"Shh! You're an idiot aren't you? If you'd only clicked the exit button we could have helped you, no one would have noticed a thing. But you had to play with it didn't you? How often does it suddenly go pitch black in the morning? Then back to daylight just seconds after?" She stared at Brad, then at Harriet. Looking as if she genuinely wanted an answer. "They know now."

"They know what?" Harriet asked.

"They know that you know."

"And who are they exactly?" Brad asked.

The old woman rolled her eyes and sighed. "It's a longer story than I have time for right now. But you need to leave here immediately for us to have any chance of catching you."

"I don't know where my clothes are," Brad replied, "but I can't go anywhere like this." The old woman just stared at him, open mouthed. "What?" He asked.

"You're an idiot," she replied "Take this and shut up." She reached down to the bottom shelf of the tea trolley and lifted out a red trolley bag, like the one she had in the park, then pushed it under Harriet's bed. Next she took a small and relatively old looking mobile phone out of her apron pocket and handed it to Harriet. "It has the code entered already, just click send and then choose exit, nothing else." She looked straight at Brad as she said the last part.

"But we already did that, we've exited." Harriet looked confused.

"No, you were spotted and caught. That's why I'm here now. Only use the phone when no-one's looking, or in an emergency."

"Now then, what's going on here nurse?" The voice came from a middle-aged doctor in a white coat. He was standing in the doorway holding a clipboard. He had an extremely tidy slicked-back hairdo and a tightly clipped moustache.

"Looks like visiting out of hours, Doctor," the nurse said with patronising disapproval.

"Indeed." The doctor looked at his clipboard for a moment, made a quick note, then after placing his pen carefully in the slot at the top, he took a wartime service revolver from his coat pocket and shot the old woman. A loud bang echoed round the room. The old woman looked surprised for a second before she imploded into a singularity at the point where the bullet hit her.

Brad looked over at Harriet and mouthed the word 'emergency' to her. But she already had the phone in her hand and was sending the message. A yellow outline of a screen appeared in front of her, with the same options as before. In an instant she reached out and touched the third option, 'exit'. Brad turned back to see the doctor raise his gun and point it straight at him. He raised an arm to cover his face, but everything went dark. There was a gunshot, but it sounded far away. The echo continued for longer than it should have, but eventually faded to nothing.

*

"No!" Brad shouted, putting his hands in front of his face. His voice caught in his throat and made him cough. It sounded strange. He sat up and rubbed his eyes. His hands and face felt oddly smooth. He was in a small dark grey box of a room. Not much compared with the last place, but again he was alone. "Harry?" His voice sounded high pitched. He coughed again "Hello, hello." Another cough to really clear his throat. "Harry!" He shouted, practically screaming the name, feeling quite uncomfortable now. He pulled away the rough khaki bed covers to reveal he was still wearing a hospital gown, not as nice as the previous one. But more alarming was the fact that he didn't recognise the legs sticking out beneath it. They were smooth and more slender than he remembered. His feet were smaller too. He became aware that a lower part of his vision was blocked by the top of his gown sticking forwards. He tried to smooth it down, only to discover something keeping it that shape. He had breasts. "Harriet!!!"

The door burst open and a tall man with a brown beard and a hospital gown ran in. "Brad, Brad, you'll never guess what... Oh," he said.

Elephant in the Room
Karen Ette

As far as I know, I am the only elephant in the house. You see, they went on holiday to Kenya and brought me home with them and I spent hours almost freezing to death in the belly of a plane. I am not very big and came from an elite group – I even have a number stamped on my bottom, but I have no idea if I am number one or number nine hundred and ninety nine, because I can't see it.

Anyway, when I arrived I was put in pride of place on the mantelpiece and lived there for a long time enjoying the attention from friends and family. The clock could be irritating at times, but I eventually didn't notice it. Then I think the same thing happened to me, I began not to be noticed and after a holiday in Spain the straw donkey took my place and I was banished to the windowsill in the dining room. Actually, I like it better here than on the mantelpiece. I was worried when the donkey arrived that I might be confined to a dark drawer or cabinet, but it's much better here; I can see loads more and enjoy watching what's going on both inside and out. In fact, I can see right down to the front gate and even know who is visiting before anyone else does, apart from the visitors themselves that is. It's interesting to watch the seasons come and go; last week I was looking out onto apple blossom and tulips, and the bluebells are beginning to colour the garden too. I'll be able to watch the father of the house, Grumpy Graham I call him, puffing and blowing as he pushes the lawnmower round every Saturday from now until October.

I do like to watch the pedestrians walking past each day. There's a young mother who pushes her pram along with a toddler in tow, probably off to meet some other young mums. Then there's the elderly gentleman who walks past each morning with his dog and when they come back the dog is carrying his newspaper in its mouth. The postman comes in the mornings, but not every day, and in the afternoons children run past on their way home from school. I haven't seen the bearded man, who wears green wellies, pushing his wheelbarrow in a while; I know when he's coming by as the wheel squeaks rhythmically as he ambles past. When he goes back the other way his barrow is always filled with vegetables. Maybe he will return soon.

It's Sunday today and preparations for the family get-together over lunch are gathering speed. I think Polly, that's the mother of the house, is cooking lamb today; it smells like roast lamb and I caught a whiff of mint sauce, yes definitely lamb. She has already started on the wine; I think that's her second glass. Oh and here comes Grumpy Graham, no doubt he'll tell her off for drinking before the clock strikes twelve, or that she could have made more of an effort; he always has to show off in front of his brother. He's making his way around the table, straightening the cutlery and checking she's put the right crystal-ware out. He makes funny guttural growling noises as he conducts his inspection; a bit like when the dog is trying to worry someone's slipper.

The doorbell has just chimed, it must be them, but I can't quite see the door today. She put me down at a funny angle after she dusted yesterday. I heard him telling her that the house wasn't fit for his brother to visit so she had to go round with her feather duster to chase all the grime away. That really tickles when she flicks it over me. Someone told her once, can't think who but it could well have been Mr Grumpy himself, that if you have an elephant in the house, not a real one obviously, then it's bad luck if it doesn't face the door. I wonder if she put me down this way, facing into the room, deliberately to annoy him. I must say she seems very calm this morning; they usually manage at least one heated exchange a day. The wine must be having a calming effect; I think she has almost finished that bottle now.

In they come, lots of air kissing and handing over of wine; there will be a few sore heads tomorrow if they get through all that. Mr Grumpy has made a grand show of making sure everyone has a drink whilst Polly's back in the kitchen; I wonder how long it will take today for him to shout for her to serve the meal. Not long it would seem, as he is ushering them to the table.

The usual seating arrangements soon establish themselves; young people at one end of the table and 'grown ups' at the other. Very soon after he calls for lunch to be served the air becomes infused with a delicious smell of roast dinner. There is a cacophony of clatter as steel collides with ceramic, interspersed with the chinking of glass and gradually subsiding to a final clunk as the last active knife is laid down onto a plate. It's taken her all morning to prepare it and they've devoured it all in minutes.

She's had to take all the dirty dishes out to the kitchen without help. After another round of drinks the smell of the roast lamb has been replaced by a lovely lemony scent – I think she's made a fancy tart for their dessert. I'm beginning to feel sleepy after seeing and smelling all that food, but the deliciousness is now ebbing away into the corners and cracks and freshly brewed coffee is the latest prevailing aroma, reclining on the room's atmosphere. The kids are beginning to get fidgety, but their slightly tipsy mum doesn't seem to have noticed. Nor has their father who is still trying to out-do his brother with talk of a new car and gauche toadying over his sister-in-law who, strangely enough, seems to be enjoying the attention.

Obviously bored with being polite and watching their parents slip into a downward spiral of inebriation, the boy-child stands up only to be told by his father to "sit down, you can leave when I say so."

"Let him go, Graham," Alexi, the sister-in-law is cooing to Mr

Grumpy and, oh my goodness, I can see from here that she has her hand on his leg and is squeezing his thigh! But he doesn't give any indication of acknowledgement and splutters:

"He can go when I say." Then a small dribble of red-wine spittle escapes his fat lips and lands on Alexi's white blouse; she is obviously pretending not to notice. "In fact," he's slurring now, "you can help your mother clear the table and wash up."

"Aw Dad," the boy-child is about to argue, but his father throws a bad-tempered look towards his wife then growls at him:

"Now, go on, do as you're told."

"But Dad..."

It's all gone very quiet and the only sounds are the uncomfortable shuffles of embarrassment. Then Polly, the downtrodden wife speaks, clearly and calmly, which is surprising after all the wine she's put away. She is talking to the boy, but looking at her husband:

"He's not your Dad," she announces.

Well, I didn't see that coming; she's really thrown him a curved ball. He soon recovers though and in an effort to make her look stupid he half slurs and half laughs:

"Well, if I'm not his Dad, who else would be stupid enough to have you?"

All eyes rest on Polly, but she doesn't afford him a reply, she just stands up, walks over to her brother-in-law and kisses him full on the mouth, then walks out leaving a clammy silence.

Looks as though I'm not the only elephant in the room.

Thank you!

If you have enjoyed Spring Tales, the authors would appreciate it if you would please take a moment to leave a review.

Also available:

Winter Tales

Amazon UK paperback
http://amzn.to/22PxTDb

Amazon UK Kindle
http://amzn.to/1pDnqfo

Amazon US paperback
http://amzn.to/1WRb4v4

Amazon US Kindle
http://amzn.to/1UTOsuM

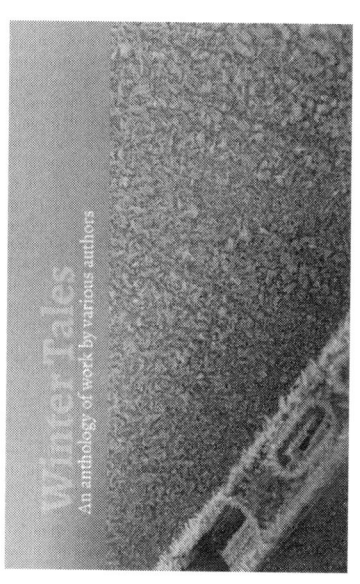

Coming soon:

Summer Tales
Autumn Tales

Ruler's Wit

A writers' group from Loughborough and Leicester who meet fortnightly to share their writing and inspire each other.

Stephen Ashurst

Stephen has a BA Hons degree in Art and Design from Suffolk College and currently works as Senior Web Designer at Loughborough University, he is also the co-owner of games company Salty Dog Digital.

He has however, been a keen writer and story teller since he was old enough to write. With an odd and sometimes surreal sense of humour, he enjoys writing stories of most genres and styles.

He has three novels on the go at present and is a member of two writing groups - Bell's Shower and of course Ruler's Wit.

www.ash28.co.uk

Karen Ette

Karen gained her M.A. in English – Creative Writing at Loughborough University and has recently completed her PhD, also at Loughborough.

She has written introductions and chapters for three books, published by Igloo, (Comfort Food, Chocolate and Harold Shipman) and has written The Advent Calendar Recipe Book, and Your UCAS Application: a step-by-step guide.

Published magazine articles include: Your Cat, The Racing Pigeon and the magazine of the Leicestershire and Rutland Western Front Association, The Tiger. She is also a member of Leicester Writers' Club and writes two blogs:

www.Battlefieldsandbeyond.com
www.FancyPansCafe.com

Melinda Ingram

Melinda gained her in M.A. in English – Creative Writing at Loughborough University. She has a B.A. in Education from the Open University and a Cert. Ed. from Brighton.

Having taught people aged two to sixty in a variety of settings, Melinda retired from the University of Leicester. She teaches English part time at a nearby F.E. College and is also a trustee of her local Community Library.

Melinda has edited and contributed chapters to books on Education for Sage and Learning Matters (under Min Wilkie) including Supporting Learning in Primary Schools and Doing Action Research. She has self-published Fictonalising Iraq in British and American Literature (Children's and Y.A.) and is working on two stories for Y.A readers.

Donna Shepherd

Donna gained her B.A. in English as a mature student at Loughborough University and has recently completed her M.A. in English, also at Loughborough.

Donna lives in North Warwickshire with her husband, daughter and three rescue cats. She is a puppy-walker for the guide dogs and is currently kept busy by Milo, her latest 'student'. A frequent character of Donna's stories is Tom the cat who in reality died eighteen months ago, and is missed every day.

Made in the USA
Charleston, SC
05 April 2016